ISBN-13: 978-1998775521

Give feedback on the book at:
lorhainneeckhart@hotmail.com

Twitter: @LEckhart
Facebook: AuthorLorhainneEckhart

Printed in the U.S.A

Edge of Night

KATE & WALKER

BOOK TWO

LORHAINNE ECKHART

Kate & Walker
The Series

One Night
Edge of Night
Last Night

Kate Sikes is just looking for Mr. Right, but somehow she only seems to attract Mr. Wrongs — and some of them are dangerous. Luckily for her, sexy detective Walker Pruett is determined to protect her...

"Mix love, attraction, and a mystery case and you have the recipe for a fantastic book!"

CAROL C.

"A quick, steamy read…chock full of romance, suspense, alpha males, and strong women."

AHERMAN

"This book was hot, hot, hot!! Without fail the characters passion explodes on the page."

A. REVIEWER

Edge of Night

Kate hasn't heard from Detective Walker Pruett since they shared a passionate night together. When he's assigned to investigate a robbery where she works, she knows she must protect her heart before she falls for him again…

CHAPTER
One

Staring off into space through the window had become Kate's pastime of late, one she wouldn't admit to anyone. She'd never been the type of woman to pine for a man, but pining was exactly what she was doing for the likes of Walker Pruett, the man who had turned a night ruined by a psychotic killer trying to end any chance Kate Sikes had of ever dating again into a night of the hottest, down and dirty best sex she'd ever had in her very young adult life. Kate was only twenty-two, and anyone would remind her she still had a lot of living and learning yet to do, but there were days she felt as if she'd lived a lifetime of bad choices, considering, when it came to men, she always picked the wrong guys.

Although Walker knew how to fuck and had driven Kate wild with a night of the kind of sex she'd never dreamed of having, he was the same as every other man she'd dated. Correction—she hadn't dated Walker, she'd fucked him, and he'd have been the first to correct her. It was sex, so she shouldn't call it anything other than what it really was.

Walker had been the detective on duty when a crazed woman had driven her car through the window of the restaurant where Kate and her date had met. The woman had headed right for her with every intention of taking her out, then had broken into her apartment to write in bright red lipstick on her wall, all because of a guy she'd met online, who, as she looked back now, hadn't been one of her better choices. No, Walker had taken her home to his place to protect her but had ended up fucking her in ways that still made her wake from a dead sleep, sweating and wanting, craving. God, how she hated him now.

It had been a month since Walker had dropped Kate off at home after her tumble down his stairs, nursing a sprained wrist, a cut to the neck, and bumps and bruises. He'd waited only long enough for her to open the door, then pulled away.

That had been the last time she saw him.

She'd expected him to call, even just to retrieve his T-shirt, which she'd worn home. It was currently washed and folded, stuffed into a drawer with her other shirts, but she pulled it out and slipped it on when she was feeling particularly lonely. Sometimes, though she'd never tell anyone, she even slept in it.

"Kate, didn't you hear me?" Keith, the front desk manager, tossed a stack of brochures on the front desk counter, behind which Kate stood in front of her computer. Her boss was a short dark-haired man with heavy brows, a round face, and a prickly attitude, and she jumped because she couldn't help feeling as if she'd been caught doing something she shouldn't have been doing. Then again, daydreaming fell under that category. Her cheeks burned.

"Yes, Keith, sorry, what do you need?" She didn't look up, instead bringing up the current check-ins and the room inventory on her screen. It was quick thinking, and she wanted to pat herself on the back, as it had kept her from landing in hot water time and again, especially as of late.

"You were staring off into space again. You need to focus on the job while you're here. Save your slacking off for when you punch out," he said in the same condescending tone he always used with her, a tone she could only put down to his need to make sure she knew her place as the assistant, not the boss. No, he was the boss, the person who could make her life easy or difficult.

She took a breath and opened her mouth to say something smart. As she looked up and across the lobby, that was when she saw him.

The panic hit her first, pulsing through her, sucking her breath out. She almost wheezed. How could she have forgotten how forbidden the man looked? He had the same short red hair and rugged shoulders, shoulders that had pinned her legs up as he rammed into her over and over, shoulders and arms she knew the feel of all too well: skin to skin in the most intimate of places.

Walker Pruett was standing not more than twenty feet from her in the lobby by the pale sofas, talking with two men, corrections cops, and damn, did he look good. She could see his badge fastened to the belt of his jeans, and his white T-shirt had her curling her fingers, as she wanted nothing more than to slide her hands over those arms, feeling the muscles flex, feeling his strength.

"Kate, are you listening to me?" Keith tapped the counter with his finger, and she felt like an idiot. At the same time, she wanted to run and hide from Walker. Of all times for Keith to be an asshole!

"Yes, Keith, I'm listening." She turned to face him, hoping he wouldn't embarrass her. He dropped another pile of brochures and papers on the counter.

"I need you to make up these kits for sales. They're short staffed today, and Shelley has calls scheduled with a group on Friday."

She couldn't believe he was passing this off on her, the grunt work he usually passed on to the front desk clerks when sales were really backed up. "Isn't this Andrea's job?" she said, reaching for the brochures and papers as the phone started to ring. She reached for it and answered. The caller wanted reservations, so she transferred it on, and Keith was still there. Maybe he was waiting for her to mess something up. As a boss, he was the worst, always focusing on what people could and would do wrong. He thrived on it. She hated that.

"Andrea is busy, and since you have all this free time to daydream and stand there looking out the window, you can put them together. It's your job when I tell you it's your job—"

"Kate."

She turned her head as Walker approached the front desk, glancing from her to Keith. She was positive her boss got off on grinding her nose into the dirt, belittling her every chance he got. Had Walker seen, heard? Of course he had. Everyone within ten feet would have picked up on Keith doing his best to make a point to Kate that he was, in fact, in charge and could make her life at work a living hell. That was a detail he had, as of late, pointed out to her on a daily basis.

"Hi, can I help you?" she said, wishing Keith would lose interest like any normal person and walk away.

Walker gave her an odd look. The way he quirked his brow, the humor or something in his expression, had her wanting to ball up her fist and ram it into his gut. So he'd fucked her and walked away, and now she was supposed to pretend…what?

She said nothing else as he tapped the counter and rested his forearm on the pale tile, his shirt doing little to hide the amazing chest she knew was waiting underneath for her touch. *Stop it!*

She squeezed her hand, fighting the unsettled feeling she knew all too well Walker could stoke inside her, making her crazy under him. She remembered what it felt like. Of course her eyes went right to that arm, seeing the shape and strength, how he had held her legs apart...

"Sir, can I help you with something?" Keith added. Kate felt her cheeks burn. She stared at her fingers, cleared her throat roughly, and tapped some keys. The screen went blank. *Shit.*

When she glanced up, Walker was looking down at her. His eyes, those amazing green eyes, were no longer smiling.

"Thanks, but I'm here to speak with Kate. Police business." His fingers tapped the badge fastened to his belt. She'd never seen him in jeans before. Maybe there wasn't a thing he didn't look good in: hot, sexy—asshole, because now Keith would be on her, thinking she'd done something illegal.

She pasted a smile to her lips, the one she reserved for guests she was anything but happy to deal with.

"Oh, I see," Keith said. "Has Kate done something I should be aware of?" He turned from her to Walker, and, of course, he was still standing there, giving her the impression he had no plans to move any time soon.

"I don't know, has she?" Walker said in a voice that made him sound so much like a man in charge. It was something she had known all too well under him, riding him, pressed against the wall or wherever he'd wanted her.

"You know what, Keith? I've got this. I'll have all the kits put together before I go today. Is there anything else?" She glanced over to Keith, and the way he watched Walker and then looked over to her, she knew he was going to pile the questions on after, maybe make her life miserable for a while. Right now, she wanted him gone so she could give Walker directions to the door.

"Sure, don't be long. You still have another two hours before you're off."

She would have rolled her eyes, but Walker was right in front of her, and she'd had enough of both these guys. "And you will have every second of my time," she added, but the moment it was out of her mouth, she realized Keith was likely to add it to his list of her shortcomings. She didn't have to look over to know, as he walked away, back into his office behind her, that he would be leaving the door open so he could hear every word spoken between her and Walker.

"I'm busy. Is there something I can help you with?" She wondered whether she could make her voice sound any more icy. She'd have loved to flip him the bird, and maybe it was the thought of doing so that added an ease to her forced smile.

"Your security footage from the cameras in the lobby and the bar for the last seven days." He gestured toward the cameras, and his expression was one she recognized: all cop. *Asshole, not even a "How are you?" or some fucking excuse for why you did the dump and run.* Had he lost her phone number? Had he suffered a head injury and been stuck in the hospital in a coma for the past month? She had to fight to uncurl her fingers from where her nails were digging into her palms.

"I see," she said. "Well, you would need to speak with Hollis McPhail, head of security." She lifted the phone and punched in his extension, staring down at the receiver, feeling Walker's gaze burning into her.

"Security," he answered, sounding as he always did: distracted, busy, as if answering the phone was a chore.

"Hollis, it's Kate at the front desk. I have a Detective Pruett out here who says he needs to see some security footage. What would you like me to tell him?" She was hoping he'd say something like "Until he has a warrant, he can go fuck himself." She would have been more than happy to relay that message.

"Fishing for something, is he?" Hollis said. She could hear noise in the background, a pen or pencil tapping on his desk. He let out a sigh of frustration.

"What would you like me to tell him?" She looked straight at Walker, who didn't seem rattled in the least. In fact, the way he watched her and then dropped his gaze to her breasts had her wanting to reach out and slap him.

"I'll be right there. Tell him to wait."

She replaced the receiver. "Hollis will be right out to speak with you."

Now what was she supposed to do? *Awkward* was all she could think when Walker still hadn't moved but seemed to be settling in. Why wouldn't the phone ring or a guest appear so she could ignore this man who'd turned her world upside down with a night of the best sex she'd ever had? Not that she'd tell him as much. No, this smug bastard probably made a habit of bedding women and tossing them away, and she was just another notch on his bedpost. She couldn't remember if she'd actually looked at his bedpost and counted the scratches.

"You're welcome to wait over there." She gestured with the flat of her hand to the sofas in the lobby that faced the fireplace. At least then she wouldn't have to keep up the smile that was beginning to ache from how hard she was forcing it in place.

"So how have you been?"

Are you kidding me? "Great, actually. You?" What the hell was she supposed to say, that she'd spent nights sitting at home, not going out, because she'd thought he'd call? How about the number of times she'd picked up the phone just to make sure there was a dial tone? She'd had to stop herself from calling him at least thirty or forty times, because she wasn't one of those girls. She'd never, ever pine away for a guy, chase him down and leave endless messages for him to call her when it was clear he wasn't interested.

"Pretty good." He was nodding, his gaze dipping again to her breasts.

She reached for the edge of her black sports jacket and pulled it over her breasts. Even though her white blouse was decent and far from low cut, it didn't hide the size of her generous bust. No, she was proud of what she had, and she didn't skimp on bras, choosing ones that added extra lift and more cleavage. He smiled as if he knew what she was doing, but he didn't stop his ogling. The man was positively a dirty dog.

"Well, Detective Pruett who's pretty good, if you don't mind, I have work to do, so if you'd like to wait over there, I'm sure Hollis will be right out." She gestured again rather sharply, and this time she didn't smile. The fact was that she didn't want to.

He didn't move. In fact, he rested his other arm on the counter, taking in all of her as if he had every right. He was a man who wouldn't accept the brush off. He was infuriating.

"What is it with you…?"

"Detective Pruett." Hollis approached and tapped the counter before she could finish, and again Kate felt her cheeks burn. She was rattled.

"You must be Hollis," Walker said, still leaning on the

counter as if he had no intention of moving. He didn't take the hand Hollis held out but instead looked and turned his head, so much the man in control, toward Kate. He winked. "Take care, Kate."

Then somehow he had his hand on Hollis's back and was walking away, far enough that she had to strain to hear. Hollis had his back to Kate, but Walker was facing her, his attention on the head of security, who was dressed in the same black jacket Kate wore, the uniform reserved for all management. He was on the overweight side, considering he spent most days glued to a desk. Whenever she saw him, he was shoveling a sandwich, donut, or whatever he had sitting on his desk beside him into his mouth.

How was it that Walker could face her from across the room and talk with Hollis, who was nodding to whatever he was saying, and Kate couldn't hear one word? She was staring at him now as he gave all his attention to Hollis.

"Kate!" Keith barked from behind her, and she jumped. "Stop daydreaming and get back to work."

When she looked back up, Hollis was walking away, and Walker was staring at her, so she picked up the brochures and papers and started sorting. When she looked up again, Walker was gone.

CHAPTER

Two

W alker had meant to call her. He'd even thought about her, Kate, time and again after dropping her off at her apartment once she'd been given the all clear from the hospital. The woman was hot and sexy, and she drove him wild on a physical level like he'd never experienced before. He'd had great sex lots of times, but being with Kate that night had been fantastic—no, scorching, so much so that he'd thought he'd died and gone to heaven.

But it was just sex. Sex with a woman with an exceptional set of tits and an ass he could hang on to. She had been responsive as all hell, too, complicated and far from submissive. She was a pain in the ass, a fiery woman. What was it about Kate Sikes that had him taking a second look? He was Walker Pruett, a detective first grade with the robbery division. He was always thinking, considering the crime and the perp, the situation, everything the victims omitted from the story—which was always key to solving the crime. This was his life, which was maybe why he'd always put women second.

Then there was Kate. She was a distraction, a nice

distraction, and he still didn't know why he hadn't called her back—or maybe he did know. Those first few days, he'd picked up on some energy, something that had him pulling at his shirt collar, feeling neediness from a woman he'd never made any promises to.

Of course, walking into the Hotel Monaco, he'd damn near crapped his pants when he saw Kate behind the front desk, staring out the window, lost in thought. It was a sad look on her face, an expression he hadn't seen before, and it bothered him.

He remembered she'd said she worked at a hotel, but he'd forgotten which one. That was something Walker never did, especially with women he bedded and up and walked away from. No, he had clear rules on that so there was never a chance of accidentally bumping into a woman he'd played with at one of his favorite haunts: something like "Don't piss where you eat."

So why was it that he had been bothered by that asshole with the dark hair making a power play with Kate? He knew it, he'd seen it, he'd done it. He hadn't had to hear what was being said. He'd been able to tell by Kate's expression, by the way the dude had been standing a little too close, telling her he could do anything he wanted. It had been ego, and the fact that the jerk had been doing all he could to belittle Kate because he was falling short in confidence it had pissed Walker off. He'd been able to tell, too, that Kate had been doing her damnedest not to let that jerk get under her skin.

Then his feet had been moving as if they had a mind of their own, right to the counter, and when she looked up at him with those deep dark eyes, so big and bold and rimmed with gold, which added an edge that matched her personality, he wondered how he could have forgotten her.

He'd rattled her. Even though he could tell she was doing her best to show him a good front, he knew when someone was giving him a phony smile—especially when there was fire blazing in her eyes for him. He found his gaze dropping to her breasts, which, by the way, were a work of art. He'd felt himself hardening there as he stood watching her, and she was doing her best to contain how pissed off she was. He knew when a woman was about to tell him where to go. He'd been given directions right to the deepest parts of hell by some of the angriest spurned women yet, but Kate wasn't one of them, although he could tell she was fighting the urge. Maybe it was down to a lack of opportunity. That had him fighting the grin tugging at his lips.

But he also had a crime to solve, a rash of robberies, and the only things in common were that the victims had been male guests of the Hotel Monaco. This was only a hunch, but Walker had a sixth sense when something just wasn't adding up, and the fact that all six men had been sucker punched and had their wallets stolen, and not one of them could identify his assailant, was also raising some pretty red flags.

It wasn't so much that they had been unable to describe who it was, it was the fact that each man had refused to report the incident. So of course Walker knew there was more to the story, a lot more.

Here he was, down at the Hotel Monaco, not only the place where Kate Sikes worked but also ground zero, in Walker's opinion, of all the trouble with these robberies. It wasn't lost on him that Kate seemed to be walking trouble. She attracted badness, heart-stopping situations where cars took out the front windows of restaurants, driven by crazy stalker women jealous Kate was after their men. What were the chances? He only considered it for a second or two before realizing the chances were really high that she was involved.

Then back to the guys, robbed not in the same place or, in fact, even in the hotel. There had been different locations: two on the street, one in a restaurant bathroom, one in an alleyway, and another at the airport. But all five victims had been men, suits or executives from different areas of expertise and industries, with only one thing in common: They had been staying at this hotel, the hotel where Kate was working, although, until moments ago, he'd forgotten that. He'd forgotten what a spitfire Kate was, as well, which was a shame, considering their encounter hadn't been that long ago. What could he say? He wasn't the dating type, the type to settle down or have a steady girl. He liked easy, no commitment, and walking away.

"So how far back does this surveillance go?" Walker asked as he took in the backroom office of the hotel, with no windows, two large computer screens, and piles of equipment. He could see the square images of different parts of the hotel, with one zooming right in on Kate, who was standing behind the front desk, stuffing papers and brochures into a folder. Did this guy have a thing for her? He glanced back down at the head of security. Definitely not the attractive buff type Hollywood liked to depict. He was the polar opposite. Maybe that worked in his favor.

"That Kate is a real sweetheart," Hollis, the security dude, said. He was busy keying in on his mega keyboard, and he had a double chin as he glanced to the screen and up at Walker. His ass was hanging over the edge of the small office chair, the kind a secretary would sit at. Hollis was a lot on the overweight side, and from the signs of the crumbs on the desk, the open box of donuts on the filing cabinet, and a garbage can stuffed full of what Walker suspected was fast food packaging, he could guess at the cause of that. The man probably didn't move off his ass very often during the day.

He grunted and wondered again if Hollis actually had a thing for Kate. The guy didn't look up again, and Walker noticed on the screen that the dark-haired boss man who'd been doing his best to grind Kate's nose into the dirt had approached her again. He was saying something to her that made the stony look Walker had seen earlier reappear. Maybe it was because he'd spent an entire night studying her body, her reactions, how she came alive from his touch as he pounded into her over and over and she screamed out under him, that he understood her reaction now. This guy was really pushing her buttons.

"Who is that guy with Kate?" he asked Hollis, who looked over and tapped the screen with the tip of his pen.

"Keith Drummond, front desk manager. Pretty much spends his days, I swear, being a pain in the ass. Takes credit for everything, basically does nothing. Shoots down every good idea from his front desk staff and then surprisingly presents them as his own. Then there's Kate. He's got a spotlight on her. She was noticed by the owner, Barry Cartwell, but then, she always receives rave reviews from guests. That didn't go over too well with Keith, which is why I suspect he's got it in for her. Doesn't want anyone working under him who'll show him up, look better than him. Unfortunately, she just can't help shining."

Why it bothered him, Walker couldn't say, but seeing Keith on screen as a pompous ass trying to make things difficult for Kate again wasn't sitting too well. A picture was starting to form in his mind of what this guy was all about. Then, he didn't have a claim on Kate. In fact, they were nothing, really. He'd taken her home to protect her and had spent a night having the greatest sex of his life before solving a crime of stalking that had turned deadly. Then he had dumped Kate on her doorstep and driven away. He had to blink at that thought, because that made him a world-class jerk. But then it wasn't as if she'd reached out to him in any way. No, she was as guilty as him. No foul could be called. They'd both had one of the best nights of sex ever. No strings, two consenting adults. No one had gotten hurt.

So why did he feel like the bad guy?

"So what about those videos?" he said. That was why he was here, after all, and he needed answers.

"You said you wanted the images from the lobby, and…" Hollis was looking up at the screen again and tapped it with his pen. Walker didn't miss the bright smile on Kate's face. A polished gentleman in a tailored suit was talking with her, and she laughed. He patted the top of the counter and leaned down as if getting ready to talk her ear off. He was striking, tall, one of those types that looked as if he had a regular schedule at the gym. His head was shaved bald and nicely shaped. Even his light frame glasses seemed to add some appeal.

"Get a lot of suits here who come into town for business," Hollis said. "Don't know how many of them are hitting on Kate. They all like her. Think a few have asked her out. So you want the bar, too, and going back how far?" He was typing again, and Walker was doing his best not to focus on the fact that Kate seemed to be flirting with this guy.

"Bar and lobby for the last week, to start."

"Okay, pull up a chair. If you can tell me what you're looking for, exactly, I may be able to help you find it quicker—"

"Stop! You'll do no such thing," someone said from behind them. The door had opened, and a man strode in.

He was about Walker's height, older, with gray hair, impeccably groomed, and he wore a dark suit, white shirt, and blue striped tie. The asshole, Kate's boss, Keith, was behind him. "Do you have a warrant, Detective?" the man asked. In that second, Walker took in the smugness on Keith's face and the way Hollis flushed. The older man snapped his finger and gestured to the screen. "Shut that down now," he said, and Hollis tapped a key and the screen went black.

"And you are?" Walker said. The older man was pulling the strings here and seemed very much in charge.

"Anthony Gersher, general manager. My front desk manager tells me you want to see our security footage. Well, until you show me a warrant, you'll see nothing." The man gestured at the blank screen.

"I don't have one, but I can get one. I'm investigating a crime. It didn't happen here, but I have reason to believe it may have started here," he said, not wanting to say anything else.

"Well, I'm sure you'll understand we need to protect the privacy of our guests, so until you get a warrant, you won't see one image from the security footage. Hollis, do you think you can escort Detective…" The man was a prick, but he knew the law well.

"Detective Walker Pruett."

"Yes, escort Detective Pruett out—and come back only when you have a warrant."

There was a moment in that exchange with the general manager when Walker realized that by the time he got back, any footage he needed to see would most likely be gone.

CHAPTER

Three

She was finished all one hundred and fifty of the sales packages, now stuffed with pamphlets and other paraphernalia, dumped on her tonight by Keith. As she glanced up at the clock, tired and hungry, her feet aching from standing for hours, she was ready to go home to an empty apartment, zap a Lean Cuisine in the microwave, and maybe finish off the tub of mountain blueberry ice cream in the freezer.

After seeing Walker, a man who had invaded her dreams every night, having her waking tired and unsatisfied and completely unfulfilled, he was now back in her head, her first and last thought and every other thought in between—exactly where she didn't want him.

She reached for her coat from the back office, which was thankfully now empty, and pulled her red purse from the drawer where she'd stuffed it. The night desk clerk, Jamie, had already arrived. He was young, dark haired, attractive, and newly married, most likely her age, with a killer smile and a way with the guests. "I'm off now,

Jamie," Kate said. "Do you need anything before I go?" She was hoping to slip out before Keith returned from wherever he'd snuck off to.

"No, I'm good," he replied. "Have a great night, Kate."

She waved and started out the front door, glancing over her shoulder to the quiet lobby, where a few guests lingered. It was dark already as she slipped on her coat, stepping out into the dry night.

"Kate."

There was something about his voice that had her feeling it right down to her toes. He got inside her the way no other man had before. Now she was mad about how he affected her. She turned and lifted her hair over the collar of her black and white coat, and it fell loosely past her shoulders.

She meant to say something smart or cutting as she took in Walker, all his rough and rugged attractiveness that she resented right now. He had pulled on a leather jacket and had it hanging open, and she took in how good he looked still in those jeans. It wasn't fair. She swallowed. "Hi…" she said, and then her throat went dry.

"You done for the night?" He was still walking toward her but now stopped, far enough away that he wasn't in her space but close enough that she could reach out and touch him. She wished he'd invade her space and take her as he had before. *Stop it!* She had to keep herself from wishing, wanting to remember how good his hands felt skimming over her skin, experiencing how good it felt to be with a man who knew how to tease her and bring her to an ecstasy she'd never felt before.

"Yes, I'm just going home." She reached into her purse for her keys even though she still had blocks to walk. It was a distraction. She looked up into those green eyes, which weren't pulling away but were taking in all of her. "So, everything all right? Did you get what you needed from Hollis?" She couldn't think of what else to ask. She wondered what he'd say. She'd forgotten how strong his focus was, giving all of himself to her. Damn him for being there now.

He didn't nod but turned his gaze away a second, so controlled, and then back to her. "No," he said.

She parted her lips to say something.

He stepped closer, and this time his hand touched her shoulder before dropping to the side and then resting on his hip. "The manager came in with your boss, Keith, to shut it down. Told me to get a warrant before seeing any footage."

She didn't know what to say. "Tony did that?" Maybe that was why Keith had been prying into their conversation. "Keith asked me what you wanted, and I told him you were meeting with Hollis to look at security footage. I don't know what the big deal is. Did something happen here that I should know? I mean, why would they stop you?"

"Good question, Kate. Seems they don't want me to see something. Gave me some bullshit line about protecting their guests' privacy."

"I'm sorry, Walker, but I'm sure if you get the warrant they'll have to show you. You didn't answer me, though. Is there something I should be concerned about? Did something happen here? Although there's no shortage of interesting things going on, I've had no reports across the front desk or even heard of the police investigating anything."

Walker was tall. He looked over her head, his hand touching her shoulder again. "You got time for a drink?"

No, she had no time for a drink. She was going home to pine away and nurse the ache inside her for wanting Walker. "Yes," she said.

Then he had her turned around and walking past the hotel, side by side. Oh, this was such a bad idea.

She was as hot as he remembered, feisty, interesting, a woman who didn't bore him. She was so complex that he could spend forever studying her and something would always surprise him. It was not just a sixth sense he had about people, it was something about Kate. Maybe that was why he'd doubled back after Hollis had let him out the side door. He had been about to go in and talk with Kate, push his luck, when she'd walked right out the front.

Only a few tables were taken at Shooters, the bar at the corner. It was a classy place as far as bars went, with music and noise in the background. He found a corner table in back and pulled out a chair for Kate. He could tell she was angry about something by the way she held herself so tightly. He sat across from her and watched as she purposely took her time slipping her coat off, setting it on the back of her chair, and tossing her hair over her shoulders. When she glanced up, he nearly laughed at the snarky look she gave him. "What?" she added for effect.

A waitress appeared beside them. "What can I get you?"

"Kate?" He gestured toward her.

"Gin and tonic," she said. "No ice, please. Oh, and could you bring the tonic on the side and I'll add it myself?" she added.

He could just imagine what the waitress was thinking, as she hesitated a second before scribbling something down. She said not a word, only sighed, most likely thinking what a pain in the ass Kate was.

"Guinness, please," he said, taking in the dark-haired young lady as she walked away.

"She was cute," Kate said.

"Who?"

"The waitress." Kate gestured and then rested her hands on the table, offering him that practiced smile, the one she'd flashed him in the hotel when he'd shown up earlier that day.

Was she kidding? He looked behind him to the waitress again. Maybe she was attractive, but she was the type that did little for him, not enough for him to remember. No, he seemed to have a thing for pain-in-the-ass women with big dark eyes and tons of attitude. He grunted.

She made a face and rolled her eyes. "What?" she said.

He shrugged. There was one thing about Kate and her mouth: He loved to shut her up, and thinking of what she could do with those lips, that tongue, had him hardening again, which was far from comfortable.

"Is there something in my hair, on my face?" She wiped her face, her big bold eyes flashing. She was fidgeting across from him.

"Why are you so nervous?"

Her eyes widened. "I'm not nervous. You just showed up where I work, and then I walked out and you were waiting there outside."

"I wasn't waiting," he said. No, he had been going back

in to see her. She was like a drug he was sure was no good for him, a distraction he didn't need right now.

She rolled her eyes. "So why am I here?"

He wasn't expecting to be put on the spot. "Because I wanted to have a drink with you. I wanted to talk to you. Tell me about your boss?" The drinks arrived, a glass with his Guinness. He picked up the chilled bottle and took a sip, waving the glass away.

The waitress set down a glass with a finger of gin and a side of tonic, lime attached to the side of the glass, napkins down. "Thank you," Walker found himself saying as he watched Kate examine the side of tonic poured in a separate glass. She lifted the lime off and set it on the table as if about to send it back. The waitress left.

"Who, specifically?" she said. "Keith or Tony?" She poured a splash of tonic in the glass and stirred with such control, tapping the plastic stick on the sides of the glass, staring at the drink. Her shoulders were back, and he couldn't help allowing his gaze to linger on her breasts. He remembered how exceptional they were to touch, to taste.

She cleared her throat as he lifted his gaze to her big dark eyes. The gold surrounding all that darkness was now blazing. She pulled at the sides of her uniform jacket, but there was no hope of covering the shapely breasts outlined through her white blouse.

He should have been ashamed, but he wasn't. "Both," he said.

She flushed. Whatever she was thinking, he wanted to know.

She cleared her throat and fidgeted, then tossed her hair again. He recognized the motion. "Keith is the front desk manager. He's a jerk, what can I say? Doesn't matter what I or anyone else does right. He always looks for something wrong, never sees the great job people are doing. He constantly cuts us down—me, mostly, come to think of it, ever since I just happened to be the one who answered a call from the owner's wife when they stayed with us. There was a maintenance problem, which I handled promptly. The missus and Brian, the owner, sang my praises, which didn't go over too well with Keith. Brian always stops in to see me now when he's here for meetings. He even ordered Keith to bring me into the last one and asked me my opinion on how to improve guest services because of the number of complaints being posted online…"

She was going on and on, rambling. She talked a lot when she was scared or nervous, too, apparently. No, she became a pain in the ass when she was scared. That was it. She was looking at him now, not talking. He didn't hear what she'd said.

"Are you listening to me?" She leaned forward and then lifted her glass to take a sip of her drink.

He was leaning back, taking in the spitfire across from him. "Go on. What about Tony? Why do you suppose he didn't want me to see the video?"

"I have no idea why Tony would say that. I know he's all about customer service, but he does favor Keith. Not sure why, since they're not related, but they're close. I remember after you left, though, with Hollis, and after Keith questioned me on who you were and why you were there, Keith left and went somewhere, which I thought was odd. You said he was with Tony and put a stop to you seeing the surveillance?" She frowned.

"What, Kate?"

She waved her hand as if it was nothing. "Maybe it was Keith who swayed Tony. Tony does seem to follow what Keith wants—not that Tony doesn't have a good head on his shoulders and think for himself. He's sharp, shrewd, but it does seem, for some reason, that Keith has his ear. For now, that is. You never know who Tony's next golden boy or girl is going to be. I wondered about that. So Tony stopped you? I don't know why. What did you say you were looking for? You still haven't told me what crime you're investigating. I'm at the front desk all the time. If you tell me what it is you need, what you're looking for, maybe I can help in some way."

She was twirling the plastic stir stick, then lifting it from her drink, putting it between her lips, and running her tongue over it. Good God, did she have any idea what she was doing with her tongue, her lips? He struggled to look away up to her eyes, and then he saw the mischief there. *Tease.*

"Robbery, all single businessmen staying at your hotel. That's the one thing they have in common, and that's not a coincidence." He lifted his beer, swallowed.

Kate appeared to be thinking as she lifted her glass again. "When did this happen?" She allowed her gaze to flicker over to him with heat—or something else.

He leaned back in his chair, sticking his leg out, brushing hers. She jumped, moved her leg away. "Over the past month, all at night. The surveillance video will give me an idea of whether they were followed. Maybe it'll show someone watching them, following them."

Kate frowned and leaned her arms on the table, then twirled the glass in her hand. "Would be kind of hard to do that, considering we'd see someone in the lobby watching, waiting. That's something I would have noticed, anyway."

"But there's the bar, too. You can't see there from where you work."

She rested the palm of her hand on the tabletop, then used her index finger to draw circles over it. He remembered how she had done the same to his chest after he'd come inside her, after he'd collapsed and rolled over and she'd rested her head on his shoulder, waiting for him to take her again.

"You're wrong," she said, then lifted the glass and took another swallow. He didn't miss the motion of her throat, where he had kissed her, ran his tongue over every part of her neck, her throat, and lower to her breasts before taking each of her nipples into his mouth. He needed to move. He was getting warm, and his jeans were uncomfortable. Hell, he was uncomfortable.

"So you're telling me what, exactly?"

"I know who comes and goes from that bar when I'm working. If someone was watching, as you're saying, and following the guests, I would notice," she said. "Or maybe not. How about you give me the names of these guys, and I can pull their information up on the computer at work, tell you more about them? I have a great memory, so if something stood out about those guests, I may be able to help."

It was perfect, even better than the surveillance. Getting access to the guest folios would give him a lot more information. "And you can access this now?" he said. In fact, it would be better than perfect. However, even though he'd considered getting Kate to help him after the fact, now he wasn't sure it was a good idea to have her so involved. "Won't this cause you a little more grief with your boss?" He'd seen the way Keith could make Kate's life hell. He was sure the guy would get off on it, and he was probably looking for an opportunity to show her the door. Walker knew he couldn't live with that responsibility, with having Kate lose a job over this. Maybe he was over-thinking it.

Kate shrugged. "Wouldn't be that difficult. I have to go back to the hotel, access the computer there." She looked at her watch. "Keith doesn't work nights. Tony should be gone, too. I can make a quick call and see." She actually reached into her purse and pulled out her iPhone.

Then he was reaching across the way, touching her hand and pushing her phone down on the table. "As much as I'd love for you to sneak me in there and access this information for me, I don't want this to come back on you," he said. "Your boss asked your security guy to escort me off the property, and he'd see me walking in with you. That wouldn't be good."

Kate didn't say a word for a second. Then there was something in her expression he wasn't sure he liked. It was stubbornness, something about her that made him realize she was going to do what she wanted. God forbid someone tried to talk her out of it.

"You can give me the names, then," she said. "Since I work there, walking back in won't draw any attention from Hollis. I can log in to the computer and check the information, and you can wait outside for me. There, easy peasy." She slid her hand across the table as if he was meant to pass her the names. She even had the nerve to appear excited, as if helping him with his investigation was interesting. "Just tell me what you need, and I'll find it."

"No" was all he said as he leaned back, trying to figure out what his next move would be.

"Fine," she said rather sharply. Then she tossed back the last of her drink and slid back her chair, getting ready to leave.

Five

She had put herself out there. She had been ready to tread the fine line of getting caught doing something she shouldn't all because Walker had asked her for help, but then he had turned her down flat. What was the matter with that man? What was his game? First he wanted her help, then he didn't. He was worse than the fickle women guys complained about, never sure whether they were coming or going, always changing their minds by the time men got them on board. Well, that was Walker. She couldn't figure him out. He was so hot and cold, grabbing her, kissing her, fucking her blind, and then nothing for how long? Here he was, being the same ass, about to walk away from her again.

To hell with that. She'd be damned if she watched him walk away again. Screw it, she was a big girl with pride. She was a catch. She wasn't going to allow Walker to decide whether he wanted her. The problem was that he was just too attractive, the best fuck she'd ever had. He was confident and strong and bossy, and she wanted him.

She stood up and grabbed her coat to leave, and she

didn't miss his expression. Oh, she was proud of herself, because he hadn't been expecting this. He didn't have to say one word about how shocked he was. It showed in his green eyes.

"What are you doing?" He gestured toward her but didn't stand as Kate looped her purse over her shoulder and her coat over her arm. She smiled down at him, feeling so much the ass kicker.

"Home, Walker. Done with games. I work hard, I'm honest, I'm a good person. I offered you my help. You sit there across from me, and one minute you want it, the next not. Do you even know what the hell you want? So I'm leaving. Goodbye," she said.

As she turned to leave, her head high, she rammed into a waitress with a tray of drinks. The waitress shrieked, and drinks tumbled down Kate's shirt, soaking it. Glass shattered on the floor and the tray clattered. Her graceful exit was now the most humiliating disaster.

She wanted to weep. How pathetic was that? "I'm so sorry," she said. The waitress was on the floor, and Kate leaned down to see annoyance staring back at her.

"Why don't you watch where you're going?" the waitress said. "Look at this mess."

"I said I'm sorry. I didn't do this deliberately…" She felt a hand on her arm, pulling her up.

"You okay?" Walker was looking down at the waitress, and he took his wallet from his jacket and pulled out some bills. "For the damage," he said.

For Kate, that was the last straw. She walked around Walker, spying the sign for the ladies' room. She didn't look back as she pushed open the door. Thankfully, the two-stall bathroom was empty, and she reached around to lock the door only to see it opening and Walker striding in.

"This is the ladies' bathroom, if you don't mind," Kate

snapped, but he didn't leave. In fact, he locked the door and then stepped toward her, and she stepped back until she bumped the single sink. Her shirt was soaked with beer, reeking from it, and then he was in her face, sliding his hand under her chin. He was touching her, his leg sliding between hers, his hand at her waistband, untucking her white blouse. How did he do this? He was so certain of himself, as if he thought she was a sure thing. He could come in here and touch her any time he wanted, and she would be waiting for him. What was wrong with her for loving the feel of his touch?

"I'm wet and sticky," she said. "Don't."

She tried to turn her head away because his face was so close, his breath so warm. She wanted his lips on her, to taste him, to be possessed by him. Walker took what he wanted when he wanted it.

"Don't what, Kate?" He ran his thumb over her lip and under her chin so she had to look up at him, but he was so close to her she could feel him. She just had to turn her head a bit more and let him kiss her. She wanted it so badly. Did that make her awful?

"I'm not easy, Walker."

His lips pulled at the sides, a smile. His nose brushed hers, and she could feel his clean-shaven face. She missed his roughness, the soft messy look of a man who hadn't shaved for a week or two. It had suited him. "No, you're definitely not easy," he said.

She hadn't meant to do it, but her lips seemed to have a mind of their own as they moved closer, or maybe it was him who had leaned closer. He was kissing her. No, it wasn't kissing, it was taking, tasting, his tongue invading her, and it was amazing.

Detective Walker Pruett was touching her, kissing her, and her body was responding as if she'd die without his touch. Her arms slid around his shoulders, his neck, and he pulled her blouse from her skirt and pulled it open. It was so rough that she heard the buttons hit the floor. She was breathing hard as he pulled back, his hands slipping her bra over her breasts, and he lowered his head, taking and tasting, his tongue circling her nipples and then nipping with his teeth. She tried to be quiet as she leaned back, her head bumping the mirror. Then his hands covered both her breasts, feeling them, running over them as if he wanted to possess her. He was peering at her, and he had to know how close she was to the edge. She knew if he walked away now, she would cry.

His hand slipped under her skirt, grabbed the band of her underwear, and ripped them off as he lifted her. Her skirt was around her waist, his hand between them, and he had a condom wrapper in his mouth. He ripped it with his teeth, and then, somewhere between her wrapping her legs around him and her shoes hitting the floor, he slid inside her fast, hard, as if he needed to be inside her. His forehead pressed against hers as he held himself there, breathing as hard as she was, as out of breath as she was. He kissed her gently once, and his warm breath brushed and mingled with hers. He still hadn't moved, pressing her against the sink, her head against the mirror. She ran her hands over his neck, the back of his head, the short red hair she loved so much. That was Walker. Everything about him she loved. Oh, God, she was in big trouble, because Walker Pruett wasn't a man any woman could afford to love. He was dangerous, and the thing he did best was walking away. The thought made her want to weep.

CHAPTER
Six

This wasn't good.

Tears glistened in Kate's dark brown eyes, turning them a softer shade as he held himself inside her. He wanted to ride her hard, to take her and drown in the softness of what she offered, but the emotion staring up at him as he held himself so still reached inside and touched a part of him he hadn't felt before.

He moved gently so as not to hurt her. The soft noise she made had him pulling out and seeing and feeling her. "Am I hurting you?" he said. He had to touch her, brushing her cheek with his hand, his thumb running over the line of her brow. The moment was so tender, with no words.

"I want you," she said, "and I'm afraid you're going to break my heart."

He moved again, he had to move, but the agony, the openness of the raw emotion shining back at him did something to his need, his selfish need for her, turning this moment with her into something he didn't want to experience. He was a "love them and leave them" kind of guy.

No strings ever. It was just sex, always. He'd made that clear. It was understood. But this was Kate. He couldn't stand the thought of hurting her, and what he was doing now was turning something enjoyable and pleasurable into something that could leave her in a bad place.

He wanted her so badly right now for sex, right? For Walker, it was all about fulfillment, instant gratification. He worked hard, he played hard. He didn't have time for messy emotional stuff.

Someone pushed on the door, but he couldn't pull away. He didn't want to. "Do you want me to stop?" he said. *Please say no.* The raw emotion looking back at him made the haze of pleasure dissolve until he was thinking. He didn't like thinking when he was having sex.

She shook her head as the emotion slipped out, and she hiccuped. "No," she said. Again, it was the raw emotion that got him. Then she leaned in and touched his lips as there was a knock on the door.

He wanted to yell at whoever it was. "Occupied, go away!" he called out, but he, for the first time, couldn't finish with Kate. What was supposed to have been just sex had changed to something he wasn't entirely comfortable with. There was something about Kate and what he was doing here with her, touching her, being inside her, exposing a tiny sliver of her heart. The one piece everyone hid from everyone else had spilled out into this moment with them.

He couldn't believe it when he pulled out, unsatisfied, unfinished. "I'm sorry," he said, his forehead pressing into hers, her warm breath on his face. He touched her face, her cheek, and ran the back of his fingers up, pulling away so he could see her expression and have some idea of what she was thinking as she clung to him. The tough girl had retreated somewhere.

"Who's in there?" There was a knock on the door again, a woman's voice. "Open up now!"

He stepped back, setting Kate down, pulling off his condom and then tossing it into the trash. He zipped up his fly and took in Kate, who was pulling down her skirt over her full hips, those hips and an ass he loved to hold on to. She slipped her white bra over her breasts and pulled at the sides of a blouse she could no longer button up, looking at the seams as if wondering what to do.

He heard the key in the lock. "Shit," he said as he pressed his hand to the door. Kate raced behind him, and the stall door slapped closed. In that second, he took in Kate's torn white underwear on the ground and her purse and coat on the small counter by the sink. The door opened, and Walker bent down, grabbed her underwear, and stuffed them in his jacket pocket. He stepped into the opening to see the waitress who'd served them as well as a man he recognized from behind the bar, holding a key, and he did the only thing he could think of to preserve some dignity and save Kate from embarrassment. He held up his badge. "Sorry, police business," he said. "Just making sure the lady wasn't injured. If you can give us a moment?"

The waitress sputtered. It wasn't her fault, of course. This was all on him. The man glanced to the waitress as if confused, and Walker ushered them both out to the hall. "The drinks, the collision. The lady was a little shaken up. If you can just give her a moment to clean up…"

"Of course, just don't lock the door," the man said, and he walked a little ways away with the waitress, speaking in hushed tones just as a woman brushed past and stepped into the bathroom. Walker leaned against the wall and waited for Kate to pull herself together and come out.

CHAPTER
Seven

He was waiting for her the moment she opened the bathroom door and stepped out into the dim hallway. She was glad for the dark wood paneling and the subtle lighting. Her coat was buttoned up, and her bare ass rubbed against the rough material under her skirt. She hadn't been able to find her underwear anywhere, and she'd gotten down on her knees to search after the other woman had left.

Even though she'd pulled herself together in the five minutes she'd sat in that stall, her legs shaking, her calm demeanor was completely rattled. She'd given herself a talking to. This was Walker, and he was all about sex. She'd been fine before, right?

Of course she wanted sex with Walker. The man was an amazing lover. He knew how to fuck like no other she'd been with. He didn't fumble around. He understood a woman's body, her needs, Kate's needs, yet he hadn't finished. He'd pulled out, leaving her unsatisfied, her heart open, bleeding and raw. Damn him for doing this to her!

He didn't say a word as she stood there, gawking like a

fool. Instead, he slid his hand over her elbow and stepped beside her. His hand slipped to her lower back without a word, and he walked her out of the bar, which was now filling up. She was wet, sticky, and aching.

"Are you okay?" He sounded genuinely caring, concerned.

"Yeah." She swallowed the lump stuck in her throat, wanting to yell at herself for how weak her voice sounded.

He stopped on the sidewalk in the darkness, a few people walking past. The streetlights were shining, and at least it wasn't raining. His hands were now on her shoulders, and he was looking down at her. "I'm sorry," he said. "You're not okay."

How could he be so damn caring? He was unsettling her now, and she didn't get rattled easily. She could think on her feet, hold it together. "What do you want from me, Walker? A quick fuck, to toss me away, walk away?" What the hell did she have to lose? She needed peace. She needed to slink away home, lock the door, and slip down into a puddle and cry for a moment before shoving back into her heart everything this man had managed in a split second to expose.

She didn't open up to anyone. It was too soon. Only fools looking for a broken heart did something so dumb, and Kate wasn't dumb. She was smart—except when it came to men.

"I don't know what the hell it is about you, Kate, what you do to me that I can't keep my hands off you." He was looking at her, his expression grim. He dropped his hands and then shuffled his stance, rubbing his hair. He winced. She wondered what he was thinking.

"Let me be clear," she said. "I hurt, I bleed. You fucked me before in one of the greatest nights of sex I've ever had. It was my fault, really, for letting you do it, for wanting it, for letting you have me, but I don't regret it. There were no promises, just sex. You said it, and I agreed, but I didn't expect the dump and run that you pulled. I wouldn't have thought I was that forgettable, and that hurts. I can't do this again. I can't be that quick fuck for you whenever you want it, whenever you show up. I'm not made that way, Walker. I want you, but you're not good for me."

Great speech. Now she had to go so he couldn't say something that would make her cry here and now, because if she started crying she was afraid she wouldn't be able to stop. She had dignity. She needed to hold her head high.

His eyes widened, and for a minute she was sure he was mad. He gestured vaguely, obviously at a loss for words.

She couldn't say anything else, so she went to step around him, to walk away home, but his hand rested on her arm to stop her. She couldn't look at him, so she stared at his hand, his arm. It was easier as she tried to hide the vulnerable part of her she allowed no one to see.

She couldn't let him. Men didn't want that.

"Look at me," he said, and his hand was so gentle on her. Why wasn't he pulling away?

"No," she said stubbornly, because she couldn't look at him anymore. It hurt too much.

He slid his hand under her chin, around her cheek, until she had no choice. She squeezed her eyes shut. Damn him for not letting her sneak away. She needed a second to pull it together, but he was giving her none of that.

"Is this what you want to see, what a fool I am?" she said. A tear slipped out as she opened her eyes. He was blurry in front of her, and she could see worry, concern, so she rested her hand on his wrist. She was weak, trembling. "I need to go home, Walker. Allow me some self-respect, and let me hold my head high as I leave. Just walk away now. Leave me be." She felt the need to go even though it was killing her, because this would be the end. There would never be anything here between them. There couldn't be. He wasn't ready, and she couldn't wait on the sidelines for the likes of Walker Pruett.

"I'll drive you" was all he said.

"No, you don't have to. I'm not that far. I'll walk," she replied. Getting into a car with Walker would only prolong the agony. Just like a Band-Aid, it was best to get it over with, rip it off quickly.

There was a scream, then someone yelling, and she looked over to see Walker go all cop.

"Help! There's a man over here in the alley." The voice was coming from beside the bar, from the dark alleyway, and then she noticed a woman and a man. Whatever they had been doing probably wasn't far from what Walker had been doing to her in the bathroom. The woman's skirt was hiked to one side, indecent, but then, so were the spike heels she was balancing on. She was one of the local hook-ers, Kate was sure, and by the looks of him as she got closer, the guy could have been anyone's husband.

"What's going on?" Walker said.

Here she had the perfect opportunity to walk away, but instead her feet seemed to have a mind of their own as they stepped away from the curb, following Walker to the edge of the alleyway the couple was now staggering out of. Looking down, she couldn't believe she was seeing a man in a pool of blood, unmoving.

This was a disaster.

He'd wanted to take Kate home before the hooker and the john stumbled from the alley—not that he'd known who they were before he'd seen them. It wouldn't have taken a detective to know what those two had been doing. He'd spotted the man's wedding ring, too, and in a split second he'd summed him up as a scumbag fucker, picking up hookers and then going home to his loving wife, who'd have no idea what kind of lowlife she was married to. The picture was coming together as he hurried to the alleyway, his flashlight pulled from his jacket pocket, shining down on the ground where the couple pointed.

"Stay here," he said to them, pointing with a sharp look that let them know they'd better listen. Then he spotted a set of legs and tan suit pants, one shoe on, the other off. A man was lying on the ground, blood on his face, head shaved, glasses broken. He wasn't moving.

Walker heard the sharp intake of breath behind him as he knelt down, his fingers to the man's neck, feeling for a pulse. There was nothing, and he glanced up and saw Kate standing over him, staring down at the man.

He stood up just as her hand touched her lips. There was shock and focus on her face as she narrowed her eyes as if thinking, staring down to the body, the man who had no pulse. "Is he dead? I know him. I was just talking to him before I left for the night," she said, touching her head. She was shaken. He knew the look all too well, having seen it far too often from victims and families after a crime.

"Yeah, I've got to call it in. Who is he?" He pulled his cell phone from his back pocket while Kate stood stiffly, her arms crossed in front of her, her coat pulled tightly, her eyes big and curious as she tucked her hair behind her ears.

"Carl Eastman, room two twelve. I can't remember offhand where he's from. Atlanta, maybe." She shut her eyes as if needing to think. She pressed her fingers to the spot between her eyebrows and then pulled them away and snapped them. "No. Shreveport, Louisiana. Atlanta is where he's originally from, where he grew up. His oldest daughter lives there. He's married, with a wife, and he has a son. I believe he said he was at Oxford, an economics major. It had to be an hour or two ago I spoke with him. He stopped at the front desk, asking about restaurants, and I gave him the list. That's something the concierge does— did. We keep a list of some of the better restaurants around. It's customer service. We strive for it, or some of us do." She was rambling.

He was still squeezing his phone, which he'd already dialed and pressed to his ear. He went to say something and stopped, because he was stunned by the information she seemed to have. She was smart, and right now she was better than any detective he could come up with. No passersby or witnesses had ever offered information like this. He had to take a second look at her as her eyes widened again, looking down on the body. Then the phone rang and connected, so he held up his hand to her and called in the homicide. He knew, as he hung up and took in Kate, that in a few moments this place was going to be crawling with cops, and every one of those cops, once they learned what she knew, where she worked, and where this guy had been staying, was going to want to take her in and pump her for the information she had on the guy.

When he looked up for the couple he'd told to stay put, he saw they were gone. "Shit," he snapped and raced the few steps out onto the sidewalk, looking up and down the street and seeing the taillights of a vehicle pulling away.

"What is it?" Kate said from behind him. She wasn't running or sounding sad or frantic or falling apart. She was there waiting for him to say something, do something.

"That john and hooker split before I could get their details, talk to them," he said.

Kate said, as she glanced up at him and then pointed upward, "But the surveillance camera from the bar, wouldn't it have picked up the couple's image? From that, can you not locate them? Considering who she was, don't you think it would be easy enough to find her? I mean, isn't there an entire department devoted to hookers and their customers? And if you find her, which I wouldn't think would be too hard, since you guys are supposed to know quite well who all the hookers are and where they are, I'm sure you most likely have her in some file, and maybe he's in your database or system or wherever it is you keep them." Then she shrugged, wide eyed. "Just saying, if you have his photo, can't you just go into the DMV or somewhere and find out who he is, too, or put his picture up on the news?"

He was looking up to the surveillance camera again

and then back to Kate. Then he looked up the street to where the hotel was, and he realized he might not need the surveillance from the hotel, after all, because what was here, on the street, which he couldn't believe he'd missed, would be better.

"Yeah, so suppose you tell me all about this Carl Eastman?" Walker said. If his hunch was right, this had most likely started as a robbery, the same case and the perp he was looking for—but this time, it had turned deadly.

CHAPTER
Nine

Kate was stuck in a shirt that wouldn't close, thanks to Walker having ripped open her blouse, leaving only one button dangling from a thread, and it was still damp, too, compliments of the bar and someone's drinks. She was now sitting in the passenger seat of Walker's sedan, parked in front of Shooters, waiting as Walker stood with the other cops at the scene, discussing the body they had stumbled upon—not just any body but that of a man she'd been speaking with hours earlier.

Carl Eastman had been an attractive man, friendly, nice. She'd flirted with him because she'd known Walker was somewhere around, and she had hoped he'd notice. She had told herself she wasn't pining away, waiting for him pathetically, when that was exactly what she'd been doing. Now she couldn't help wondering, as she took in Walker and the other cops at the scene, whether this sense of surreality and darkness was normal for him.

She noted the glances her way, the curious stares. Walker had ushered her into his car as soon as the first unit arrived on scene, telling her to stay put. It wasn't lost on her that he wanted to separate her from what was going on. He was an enigma, and it left her wondering whether he had any idea of the mixed signals he continually threw her way: wanting her and not, pulling her and pushing her away. It was enough to make her head spin, but if this was his life, no wonder he was the way he was.

There she was, sitting like a good girl, doing what Walker Pruett had dictated, again.

"No more," she said as she squeezed her purse, reached for the door, and opened it. She stepped out onto the sidewalk as several pairs of eyes all turned her way. Then Walker was moving her way, so she gave him her back and, with a flick of her wrist, shut the door. Her hand went to the neckline of her coat as she slipped the strap of her purse over her shoulder and took one step. He reached her, this time holding her arm, not letting her go. It wasn't gentle, rather something a cop would do.

"I told you to stay in the car. Can't you for once just do one simple thing you're told?"

She stared at his hand and then back up to him. He wasn't smiling at all. He appeared very much the pissed-off cop she'd first met, the distracted one in the restaurant the night of her blind date, when a crazed woman had driven her car through the front window. This was the distant man she wanted, the one she shouldn't want, because he wasn't needing her, loving her, the way she needed.

"I'm going home, Walker. You have your little murder here to solve. I need a shower. I'm sticky, damp, uncomfortable. I reek." She could smell the beer, the stench as she patted his hand, which was still holding her arm.

Then he was shaking his head. "You're not going anywhere, Kate."

Oh, now he was pissing her off. "If you think you can

tell me where and when I can leave, you are mistaken. I'm going home, so kindly take your hand off me."

"Kate."

She glanced over to see a short female cop, on the heavyset side, her hair color a shade darker than Walker's. It was Kruso, whom she'd met while naked, hiding behind Walker after the best shower sex she'd ever had.

"Hi," Kate replied. She was usually more chatty, but there was something about the way she was feeling now: hurt, vulnerable, mad at a man who knew how to push all her buttons. "I'm going home. If you two will excuse me…"

She went to take a step when Walker had a hold of her again. Kruso gave Walker an odd look and said, "You didn't tell her?"

"Didn't have a chance yet."

"Tell me what?" Kate was now tired of this.

"You have to come down to the station. This is now a homicide, and because of the details you know about this guest, Medina and Weber want to talk to you," Walker said.

"What?" Maybe she didn't believe him, as she looked to Kruso, who was now looking up at Walker. Whatever it was that passed between them, Kate was positive there was way more to what was going on than Walker was saying— and it seemed he wasn't about to share any of it with her.

Scorned women weren't completely unfamiliar to Walker. In fact, they were the type of women Walker was intimately familiar with, only because he seemed to excel at steering the women he was involved with—no, the women he fucked—down that particularly hostile road. It was a trait of which he wasn't particularly proud.

Kate had said not one word since her shriek when he'd tucked her into the backseat of his car and shut the door so she couldn't get out. Her hands pressed to the glass, her eyes flashing in a way that let him know he'd gone too far. Even Kruso couldn't believe he'd done such a thing. As he climbed in and looked back at Kate, she refused to look at him. She said not one word as he drove to the station in silence, the tension filling the air between them. There was a point when he looked back that he wanted to stop and say he was sorry, maybe move her up front. He'd even tried to talk to her. He thought about explaining his reasons, that he was just trying to keep her safe. She had to know that, to understand, but she was stubborn instead, staring straight ahead, refusing to look his way—refusing to answer him.

When he pulled into the station and backed into a spot, he expected her to soften a bit. Boy, was he wrong. In fact, when he opened the back door to let her out from where he always stuffed the bad guys, though Kate was far from a criminal, he realized she'd taken the silent treatment as time to suddenly stick that wall up between them, concrete reinforced with steel, and he was positive she'd have told him with very detailed instructions how to go straight to hell.

She walked beside him into the station, stiff and angry. As he stopped to pick up messages from the desk sergeant, she said, "I'd like to make my one phone call, please." He couldn't believe she'd come up with such a thing.

Fabriski, older, balding, and insistent on doing a greasy combover to hide the baldness, gave Walker a lost look, and all he could do was shut his eyes for a second as he sighed.

"Ah…" Fabriski was looking to Kate again and then to him when Walker shook his head and reached for Kate's arm.

She promptly shook him off and gave him a look that practically snapped, "Drop dead." He lifted his hands in surrender, stepping around her, trying to get a sense of how deeply pissed off she was, and he didn't miss the expression on Fabriski's face.

"A suspect?" he said.

Walker shook his head. "A material witness." He gestured with his open hands again in surrender to Kate. "Look, I'm sorry, I shouldn't have stuck you in the back seat the way I did," he said as they started walking again.

She, of course, said nothing as she moved far enough away that he could feel the air between them. He knew that if he touched her, she'd likely deck him, which would land her in a lot of hot water, considering where they were, even if she was entirely in the right. She didn't answer, though. She didn't even look his way. In fact, she lifted her chin higher.

"Kate, please, would you give this little attitude of yours a rest?" he said as he rounded the corner into the bullpen and ushered her over to his desk, up against Kruso's. He remembered the comment she'd made under her breath after he'd stuck her in the back seat, something about him needing help, and he was pretty sure she had been referring to the psychiatric kind. He gestured Kate to the empty chair beside his desk, and she looked at it and sat.

"Can I get you some water, something to drink?"

This time she did look at him. Her lips were tight. Her expression was mutinous. She gripped her purse against her chest tightly as if she was expecting someone to rip it away.

"No, thank you—just my phone call, please," she added, and he knew right now that of all the things he'd done, he wished he could go back and undo how he'd treated her. She was about to walk off, and he knew Kate could be stubborn and pigheaded. How could he tell her that the other detectives, after learning where she worked, would have her inside the hotel, risking her job to get them the information they wanted and needed to complete their investigation? No, Kate deserved to be protected. How could he make her understand?

"Look, there's a lot you don't understand," he said. "I'm trying to protect you."

Wow, her expression could have landed a man in the burn unit.

"I understand perfectly," she said. "You made yourself

clear when you tossed me into the back seat of your car as if I were nothing more than a common criminal, sitting in the same spot people you've arrested have sat countless times. It's good to know you think so highly of me, Detective, especially considering a few moments earlier you followed me into the ladies' bathroom, pressed me against the glass, and tore off my underwear, which, by the way, I couldn't find." She growled the last part in a loud whisper as she leaned forward a bit. "And you did your best to show me once again that I can't pick a guy if my life depends on it. No, I'm doomed. Seems to be a family tradition, first my mother and then me—"

"Oh, for the love of God, Kate, stop. You understand nothing. Maybe I shouldn't have stuffed you in the back, but you can be so damn infuriating at times. Do you have any idea how valuable you are to this investigation? Those homicide cops would not only encourage you to put your job in jeopardy by sneaking into the hotel and opening your files to give them information on all those past guests, but they would expose you to unnecessary danger. That guy," he said, looking behind himself to the cops in the bullpen, talking on phones and to each other, some walking in and out, "that guest who was murdered, he had been robbed with the same MO as the last five victims staying at your hotel. From what I could tell in the few seconds I had at the scene while trying to keep an eye on you at the same time, whoever is doing this has just bumped up their game from thief to killer." He hadn't meant to scare her, and when her face paled he wanted to reach over and touch her, but he was stopped when the two homicide cops at the scene walked into the bullpen, heading right toward Kate. "Ah, shit," he said.

"Walker, heard you slipped off with the witness," Medina said. He had a thick mustache, brown hair that needed a cut, and sharp blue eyes, and he wore blue jeans and a dark jacket. His partner, Weber, gestured to Kate as he walked past, dressed in dress pants and a dark suit jacket, as well. His tie was pulled down, and his dark wavy hair was highlighted with streaks of gold. At times, Walker wondered whether they were natural. Weber knocked on the captain's door and popped his head in, then glanced back once. Kate seemed to be taking all of them in, and she was thinking. That definitely wasn't good.

"No, I didn't slip off with a witness. I left with my girl-friend," Walker said. He could immediately feel Kate's eyes burning into him again. This time he knew he'd thrown her a curveball, and she was scrambling. Hell, even he was trying to figure out why he'd said such a thing.

Medina smiled and glanced down at Kate, whose gaze hadn't left Walker's. "You always stuff your girlfriend in the back of your car like some common criminal?" he said, turning to Kate. "You let him treat you this way, honey?"

She opened her mouth to speak, then shut it, and to Walker, that was priceless. He'd managed to turn Kate Sikes speechless.

CHAPTER
Eleven

Having Walker tell someone she was his girlfriend when, up until moments ago, she had been expecting him to walk away once again had Kate feeling like the punchline of some big joke. Here she was, sitting at his desk. Seconds ago she'd been fit to be tied because he had treated her like a common criminal, and now she'd suddenly been upgraded. So how the hell was she supposed to get her head around the fact that Walker Pruett was telling another man, a detective who'd made a beeline straight for her, a fact she hadn't missed, that she was his girlfriend, that she was no longer someone of no importance but someone who mattered in his life?

She sat back in the chair and crossed one leg over the other, very aware of her bare ass under her dark skirt. She wondered whether Walker realized the same thing, as he was staring at her, his eyes narrowed, taking in her legs, running his gaze up and down as if letting her know his stamp was all over her. She just smiled up at the detective glaring down on her, and he looked back at Walker.

"I need to speak with your girlfriend about the victim."

"Carl Eastman was a guest staying at the hotel where I work," Kate said, "the Hotel Monaco. I was just speaking with him a few hours ago." She lifted her wrist to look at her gold-plated watch with its black leather wristband, a gift from her father. She noted the minute hand ticking by, coming on eleven—to be exact, six minutes to the hour. "It would have been around seven thirty. Nice man, checked in yesterday, here on business. Not sure what else I can help you with or what you'd like to know about him." She tapped her fingers against her leather purse. Her nails were clipped short, with chipped clear polish. She needed to clean them up.

"Kate," Walker said in a voice that sounded suspiciously like a warning, but she was way past taking any kind of warning from him. Right now, she was all about pushing every one of Walker's buttons, whatever would set him off so he felt as rattled as she did.

"Yes, Walker?" she said in a voice so sweet that even to her own ears it sounded like she was testing him.

His eyes darkened. "Kate was with me, so there's no reason for you to be speaking with her. Everything she saw, I did, so talk to me."

"I disagree," Medina said. "I think Kate could be a great help, considering this case is linked to yours."

"Possibly linked to mine," Walker said.

Medina let out a dry laugh. The way they were talking to one another other, she wondered if they'd forgotten she was here.

"Walker, if I can help and provide information, why wouldn't I?" Kate said, gesturing between the two cops, who looked about as friendly as two dogs circling the same bitch. She wondered for a moment whether she should introduce herself properly, maybe hold out her hand. If they worked with Walker and she was now suddenly his girlfriend, she should introduce herself, or Walker should have. Maybe doing that would push Walker even further to the edge. She didn't know why it pleased her to see him angry, unhinged, rattled.

"You can't," he said. "You were with me at a bar having a drink, and we were leaving when a hooker and john stumbled out of the alleyway. They took off after. Whatever information Kate has from the hotel, I also told you that until we have a warrant, as per the general manager, we're not getting anything, and Kate can't help. Go into the bar and focus on the surveillance. Find that hooker and john. Start with them."

Medina was shaking his head. He wasn't smiling, and even Kate knew that was something he should have been all over. "We'll do that. Already have technicians pulling the surveillance."

"But Kate still has a lot to share. I think helping is up to her," Medina added, and Kate didn't miss how loud they were being. Everyone was looking, and then Kruso, the redheaded cop she liked, strode across the room to the desk facing Walker's and took in all of them. She looked over to Kate again as if she could possibly shed some light on whatever was going on with the two men.

"No, it's not up to Kate, and I'm telling you to back off," Walker said. "You're not talking to her here, now, or anywhere. In fact, we're leaving, Kate." He was now standing and took a step toward the other cop. Medina stepped closer to Walker, almost nose to nose, and Kate wondered for a minute whether a fistfight was about to break out. She hoped not, but this was rather exciting.

Never had she expected Walker Pruett to not only call her his girlfriend but also dictate whom she could talk to. At the same time, he looked about to fight to keep her out of an investigation she was more than willing to help with.

She liked Walker, and though this was unsettling in a flat-tering kind of way, it was something she'd secretly longed for.

She glanced back at Kruso, whose expression seemed guarded, as if she was about to jump into this pissing contest and separate the two detectives. She also seemed to have caught on to what Walker was insinuating about Kate, so Kate leaned back, relaxed a bit, and turned her head, smiling over to Kruso. "So is Walker always this cooperative at work?"

"Kate!" Walker barked, reaching for her hand and yanking her up before anyone could say anything else to her. He pulled her with him, bumping into Medina as he moved her away.

"Sorry," she said to Medina as she moved past, Walker still holding her hand. His fingers, strong and rough, were linked with hers.

"Walker!" A man shouted from behind them. She noted his expression, grim and irritated, as he turned.

"Shit," she heard him say before he looked down at her. "Do me a favor: Say nothing to anyone unless I'm sitting in the room with you, understand? Listen to me this time, Kate."

She frowned and began to open her mouth when Walker put both hands on her, ushering her back to his desk. He gestured to Kruso and then walked away into an office with the other detectives and an older man, who was short and rounded in the middle. Whatever was going on, she realized that for some reason Walker didn't want her speaking to these cops. For the life of her, though, she didn't know why. Talking to them would most likely clear up his case and solve the homicide of a guest she'd met and liked. If she could help Walker, why in the world wouldn't she overcome every obstacle to do just that?

Twelve

Who was Kate talking to now? He wanted to race to the door of the captain's office. He couldn't help keeping an eye on Kate from where he stood, making sure he had a view through the captain's window into the bullpen. The two dickhead detectives from homicide had already gone in, whining about how Walker was keeping a material witness who had vital information that would not only lead them to whoever had killed the guests of the Hotel Monaco but also tie them to the recent robberies, maybe. Walker was really pushing the idea that this was a reach.

"Look, I already told you I went into the Hotel Monaco, tried to get surveillance footage. The GM sent me walking, said to get a warrant, and I'm going to get one. Kate is just a front desk clerk. She knows nothing. I'm not putting her job and reputation at risk."

"I doubt very much she knows nothing," Medina said. "She was very helpful, seemed to have a wealth of infor-mation to provide. I think you're holding out, Walker, maybe trying to solve this yourself, take the credit. We all know you're not a team player." He paced, rubbing the back of his head, and Weber also looked as if he wanted to throttle Walker.

"And she's his girlfriend," Weber said, tossing out the information to the captain.

"Didn't know you were seeing anyone, Walker," the captain said. "That makes it a little sticky. Nevertheless, if she has information on a crime, we need to talk to her. You know that."

"No, she doesn't, as I told Medina. Kate and I were next door at the bar. We just stumbled across the guy in the alley. She knows nothing of the murder or what happened. It was that hooker and her customer in the alley with him. Focus on finding out who those two are. Find them, talk to them. Maybe they're the ones who're behind the robberies and killed that man. Maybe the crimes aren't even related." Even as he said it, though, he knew it wasn't true. In his gut, from the moment he'd seen the body and learned the man was a guest at Kate's hotel, he'd just known the crimes were similar—and it wasn't any one thing. It was everything: where the body was, the alleyway, the time of night, and the fact that the man had been wearing a suit. In every one of his cases, every man robbed had been wearing a suit.

"Yes, do that," the captain said, gesturing to the two detectives.

"We're already on it. We'll find them, haul them in, and talk to them, but Walker's girlfriend is here now, available, and ready to talk. She wants to help." It was Medina speaking, the asshole, who wouldn't hesitate to toss Kate right into the path of an oncoming bus if it meant he got his case solved. Walker had seen it time and again with cops, the way they pretended to have a witness's best interest at heart, but it was really all about their own gain.

Hell, no, it wasn't going to happen to his Kate. There he went again. She wasn't his, not really.

Now the captain seemed to be wondering about a lot of things, shaking his head at Walker as if he knew what he was all about, what he was trying to do. "Sorry, Walker. I understand, but they're talking to her, and Kate could also shed some light on things. Talk to her. See what she can offer."

Walker was having none of that. He was shaking his head. "You're not talking to her. Whatever she knows you can get from me."

He'd gone head to head with his captain a time or two, and this wasn't something he could win. He knew that, but he'd be damned if he let Kate get dragged into something that could put her in a bad spot. He didn't want that for Kate, not after what he'd done to her.

"Captain, this is a material witness," Medina started. Weber said nothing as he glanced out the window to the bullpen, and Walker had stopped listening, because Kate, who moments ago had been parked beside his desk, chatting away to Kruso and whoever else had walked up, was now gone.

Shit, where did she go? "Listen, Captain, she isn't a material witness," Walker said. He had to get out of there and find her.

"She can get us information inside that hotel," Weber insisted.

"No, she can't."

"Well, why not?" The captain was sounding irritated. No, this was the point he got to when Walker pushed him, but he did that often with every one of authority. It was his downfall, his Achilles' heel, he was sure, and something he didn't want to examine too closely, along with his fear of intimacy and allowing a woman to get close. *Shut up.*

No, Walker at times toed that fine line, and if he wasn't as good as he was, he'd probably have been tossed out on his ass long ago for being difficult and impossible to work with. He just couldn't help himself from being the smartass cop who couldn't and wouldn't keep his mouth shut. But right now this all came down to his boss siding with these two pricks, and he didn't like that one bit.

"Because I don't want Kate involved," he said. "She's nice, I like her, and she doesn't know these two assholes." How could he tell them that the real reason was because he felt like a first-class jerk after the way he'd treated her? He'd never considered her feelings before, and maybe he was doing a little overkill now.

His boss gave him a look, letting him know he wasn't going to win this one. "Walker…"

He knew where this was going. "Fine, but I'm there in the room, part of this. You don't talk to her without me. She goes nowhere without me."

He went to the door and pulled it open before his boss could kick him out, tell him no, or assign him somewhere else. If that happened, he'd be on the phone to one of those scumbag lawyers he loved to hate, getting someone down here to protect his girl for him. He turned in the doorway, gripping the frame. "After this talk, I'm taking her home," he said—that was, after he found her.

"Five kids, and look at them," Kruso said.

Kate was holding the photo Kruso had pulled from her wallet of her very tall, lean husband, with glasses and an oval face. Their five children looked to range in age from a toddler to a teenager, and every one had Kruso's red hair.

"Oh, they're so cute," she said. They looked like a handful, she noted from the gleam in the boys' eyes. She touched her chest for a minute, struck with an image of Walker's child with the same impossibly challenging personality, and she ached again.

"I think so, but I'm partial. After all, they are my kids, and isn't it a parent's responsibility to think her kids are the best looking, the greatest, better than any other kid out there, even though they're a handful? Some days police work is the easy job. I sometimes race out my front door breathing a sigh of relief because I've escaped the madhouse." She laughed.

Kate handed the photo back to Kruso, who set a

steaming mug in front of her where she'd tagged along into the cops' break room. There was a small fridge and a coffee pot. She didn't want the coffee, but she wanted something: company, someone to talk to so thoughts of Walker wouldn't keep invading her, as they were now. She was still trying to figure him out.

"Aren't you hot? Why don't you take your coat off?" Kruso gestured.

Kate placed her hand to the neckline where her coat was buttoned to make sure it was secure and didn't show. Of course she was warm. Anyone could see that. "Stain," she said. "I'm good, though."

Kruso lifted the lid on one of those bakery boxes someone had stuffed by the coffeepot. She lifted out a donut hole covered with enough sugar Kate would have been dizzy and most likely close to a diabetic coma if she'd eaten it. Her broad hips would also be that much wider. No, safer to say no, stick to this evil brew sitting in front of her.

"Donut?" Kruso lifted her hand toward Kate, offering. "Seems to be no shortage here. Someone always has to arrive at work with a box. Not sure whose turn it was this week, but today it looks like donut holes." She was digging in the box, and Kate took in her big ass, wondering if she had any idea what all that fat, refined flour, and sugar was doing to her. "Oh, look, there's a jelly donut left!" She held it up. "You sure you don't want one?" She licked the white powdered sugar from her fingers.

Kate just shook her head, lifting the mug of coffee, which smelled stale and bitter. She could imagine it would probably go down like tar after how long it had been sitting in the carafe. "No, all yours." She blew on the steaming brew and sipped, her eyes burning. So was her stomach, now. The coffee was worse than it smelled.

Kruso was leaning against the counter, taking a giant bite of the jelly donut she'd found. Some of the purple jelly inside dripped on her chin. She wiped it with her finger and shoved it in her mouth. "Mmm, yum. This is the kind of thing I can't have in my house. The boys would be hanging off the wall, so this is my guilty treat at work." She was talking as she crammed the rest of the donut in her mouth. "So Walker said you're his girlfriend. Didn't know he'd been seeing you, but then, Walker, as you would know, doesn't share much." She was brushing the crumbs from her beige long-sleeved shirt.

Kate was still holding the mug, staring up at Kruso. The woman was sharp. She knew what Walker had done. Kate shrugged. "Happened kind of fast."

Kruso was shaking her head. "Happened before he even knew it, I figure. But that's men for you. Sometimes it takes a baseball bat upside the head for them to figure out what's been sitting right in front of them all along." She reached in the box to grab another donut hole and held it up as if examining it. "Yeah, Walker had a thing for you from the beginning. Saw it that first night I met you, when he thought something had happened to you. You should have seen the fear of God it put in him. I said to myself, 'Well, that's a girl who's going to keep things interesting for Walker.' He's the kind of guy who gets bored easy. Works all the time. His free time consists of taking home his cold cases and going through them in detail to see if there's something new he missed. I thought, wow, maybe he'll even start to work better with others, you know, seeing you and all..."

"Stop it," she said. She had to interrupt, because she knew Kruso was smart and had to know the bullshit Walker had just dished out. For Kate, listening to this was now downright painful. "You already know that we weren't seeing each other. Well, we were, but I hadn't heard from him until he walked into the hotel tonight where I was working. I damn near had a heart attack seeing him there, and then when he walked over..." She had been over the moon, seeing him, and that had made her angry.

"You wanted to slug him, didn't you?"

She took in the big smile on Kruso's face. "You knew."

Kruso was still smiling, nodding. "Walker has a history of loving them and leaving them. Hoped he had changed, knew he hadn't when I asked a few times about you and he said nothing. I knew he'd never reached out. I hoped you'd call, and I never heard one way or another if you had." She gestured toward Kate. "And now look, you're his girlfriend."

"After he shoved me in the back of his cruiser," Kate added, because it smarted to know he would do such a thing to her.

Kruso shut her eyes, shaking her head as if she understood this enigma of a man better than most people. "One of his dumber moves, but you're also a woman who can twist Walker up in knots and make him act crazy like I've never seen before. You'd gotten your hooks in him. He just hadn't figured it out yet—or apparently he had." She gestured out the door.

"If you know Walker so well, tell me, what was that, anyway, between him and that other cop?" Kate was stumped still. It seemed as if he was bashing heads with almost everyone.

"Turf, and a pissing contest. Walker didn't like the fact that Medina wanted to speak with you. He was making it clear you're his, a guy marking his territory. It happens slowly to some, but when it hits, watch out."

"In order to be his, it has to be mutual," she said. After wanting Walker so badly after all this time, she should have been ecstatic to be called his girlfriend, but the problem was that she didn't know how long it would last, and when he dumped her off in front of her place again and drove away, she could already feel the loss. Would that be it, the last time she would see him?

CHAPTER
Fourteen

"There you are." Walker strode in. "I told you to stay put. Can't you listen just once?" He was in her face as Kruso walked out, shaking her head.

"No, you told me not to talk to anyone," Kate said. Of course she knew exactly what he'd meant, but she loved to butt heads with Walker. Stirring him up was one of her favorite pastimes. "But I didn't really listen to you," she added with attitude. She hoped that would stir Walker's anger, and she realized as she sat there that she loved his fire, his passion, his fight. He was a man who interested her, a man she'd never be bored with. He was one of those rare complex males who could love her deeply or crush her. She also knew that. What would it take for him to let her in?

She was sitting there in the hard plastic chair, still holding the mug of godawful coffee.

"You really drinking that stuff?" He gestured and made a face.

She pushed the mug away. "No, it's horrible. I don't know how you can drink this."

"It's a requirement to be a cop: long hours and shitty coffee." He reached down and moved the mug away from her before reaching for her hand and pulling her up. He stood closely, reaching his other hand out and touching her face. She wondered for a minute whether he thought he had to do this. She sensed something in his touch that bothered her.

"About earlier," he started.

She could make it easy for him, but that wasn't going to happen. "Yes, Walker, what about earlier?"

"What I said to you about…" He gestured between them, and it took only a second to realize he was having trouble talking about her being his girlfriend. It was a thing, she supposed, with some guys, as if they were being suffocated. The thought of being tied down to just one woman was freaking him out.

"I'm not holding you to it, Walker, so stop worrying about it. You called me your girlfriend, and now your eye is practically twitching. You're trying to figure out how to get out of the jam you got yourself in. It's painful, so I'm going to help you out."

He was still holding her hand, but she could feel the change in grip, so she squeezed his hand gently and covered it with her other one, patting as if comforting him. Then she pulled her hand away.

"You can get that freaked-out look off your face right now," she said. "You want to tell these guys I'm your girl-friend because of whatever territorial thing you've got going on, fine." She poked his chest. "You do that, I'll go along with it. Then you can have someone drive me home. You don't have to spend one more minute with me. And… well, have a nice life."

She took in the shock or something in Walker's expression. Whatever it was, the man was speechless. He opened his mouth to speak when the other detective, the one in the suit, came in, and for the first time since being with Walker, Kate felt she was the one in control.

"Kate, my name is Weber, detective on homicide," the detective said. "I understand you have a wealth of information you could provide us to help shed some light on some of those guests who stayed with you and got robbed, and this guy tonight who was killed, Carl Eastman. Preliminary results just came in from the coroner on scene. He died of blunt force trauma, repeated blows to the head, temple. It appears he may have fought back, got some skin under his fingernails. He's some executive from a pharmaceutical company in Louisiana."

Kate held out her hand and actually smiled over to Weber. He was the suave, better-looking one of the two detectives, the one with the nice hair, nice smile, which he flashed at Kate. She smiled back, and Walker wanted to snarl.

"Shreveport, Louisiana," she added.

Weber faced Walker. His expression virtually yelled that Kate was a gold mine. He was still holding her hand, and she was letting him. "Shreveport... So you work at the hotel where Mr. Eastman was staying?"

He was pumping her already, and Walker was struggling to find his footing after Kate had just yanked the rug out from under him. She'd cut him loose, saving him from figuring out a way of ending whatever this was between them, and he didn't like it. It wasn't supposed to happen like this. He was the one in charge, the one who handled, maneuvered.

"I'm the assistant front desk manager, so I see all reservations, check in guests, take care of all their requests, see who's where, doing what. I hear the fights, the complaints, who wants the extra towels or thinks the room's too hot or cold. I could go on all night about the odd things people do in hotels, and I know all of it. All the other departments' reports go across my desk: housekeeping, food and beverage, the night clerk. Well, Keith, my boss, sees them as well because he's the front desk manager, but there isn't much he sees that I don't see first. I pretty much know maybe more than he does about all the guests: where they're from, quirks they have, you know." She shrugged. "And all those intimate things you're not supposed to know."

She was flirting with Weber, and Walker couldn't believe how Weber was enjoying this. Both Kate and Weber were now acting as if he didn't even exist—which he did!

"Shit, Walker, you were wrong about this one," Weber said. "Sounds to me like Kate here could provide us a wealth of info that would practically giftwrap who did this."

Kate had no idea what she was doing. He wanted to stop her. He needed to pull her aside and stop her from talking, get her to behave. Now why did that sound like an impossible task?

"So then you'd know the guests' interests?" Weber said.

"Oh, sure. You start to read people pretty well, doing what I do." She waved her hand and laughed. "People always come to the front desk when they need something. We're kind of like their gateway, so we get a pretty good idea, especially at check-in. Weary travelers on edge are less likely to hide who they really are."

"So what exactly is it that Mr. Eastman liked, wanted to do for fun? Tell me some of the things he did."

"He's more of a foodie, wanted names of some of the

local restaurants, good ones. He had a fondness for hot and spicy, so I sent him over to the Cavalier, the Vietnamese place. He stopped to thank me tonight for the recommendation. Apparently, it had become his favorite restaurant." She smiled brightly, not at Walker.

What was he now, odd man out?

"Any other things he liked to do? Meetings he had, places he went?" Weber now was scribbling notes in a notebook he'd pulled from the inside pocket of his jacket.

Kate frowned, and tiny lines formed between her eyebrows. She tapped her lip with her finger. "You know what? He had two meetings, one yesterday, another today. He was gone most of the day. He was in the gym in the morning, and some of the housekeeping staff carried on about how good he looked. He was a man who worked out, and apparently he used all the equipment in the gym and then ran for what one of the housekeepers said was twenty minutes." She shrugged this time, making no excuses as she looked right to Walker. "Girls notice these things." What was she saying?

"Anyway, he was all about his meetings and the gym. He went to the restaurant alone for breakfast. Other than that, he was the perfect guest," she said, raising her eyebrows, her excitement showing as she glanced over to Walker again. Maybe she was testing him, daring him to do something to stop her.

"So you have access to guest information, past and present?"

"Oh, uh-huh. That's easy. I just pull it up on the hotel system. I can tell you anything you want to know, their home addresses, the cars they drive, the rooms they're in. Housekeeping has loads of stories about guests, too. After all, they see all their intimates, personal belongings, when they go into a room to make it up. And then there're those that overspend. We always know because they're the ones whose credit cards decline. I can't believe the number that still insist they want to pay cash. You'd be hard pressed now to find any decent place willing to take it. Credit is credit. Cash always raises red flags."

She was going on and on, and Weber was scribbling as fast as he could during Kate's spiel. He was trying to figure out where to stop her. Walker knew Kate would go off, and he knew how to stop her, too, but there wasn't a chance in hell Weber was going to learn anything about how to soothe Kate, to keep her focused, to keep her calm.

"Okay, stop," Walker said. "I told you there's no way in hell Kate is accessing that information for you." He moved, sliding his hand around Kate, grabbing her ass, pulling her with him.

She squeaked, and he knew it was from his hand. The placement was totally inappropriate, but he knew the moment Weber understood his meaning. Walker didn't let Kate go as he moved her away, keeping her in his space. He reached for both her arms, holding her still, and he could tell she was affected by him by the way she struggled to breathe calmly. It was in her expression, her eyes, how tightly she held herself. He knew she was fighting him, but it was a losing battle, and he wished to hell that Weber would leave so he could work Kate down to putty in his hands. It was so wrong, yet he was willing to stoop to anything to get her to stop being so helpful.

"You're not going back into that hotel to access any details until I get a warrant, and then I'll make sure you're kept out of this. Seriously, Kate, you can't risk your job. You know what will happen. I saw how that twerp Keith had it in for you. He's just watching, waiting for you to do something you shouldn't, and I can't protect you from that. He'd have every right to fire you, to have you walked out and make sure you never work again in the industry, put the word out, destroy your credibility." He knew the moment she understood what he was saying. When she glanced down, it had finally sunk in.

"Well, so be it," she said. "If it will help solve a crime and prevent anyone else from being attacked or hurt or worse, then of course I'll go in. And you're wrong, no one will know. I'll go back in tonight. Keith will be gone, Tony will be gone. It's just the night staff, and no one will question that I'm there catching up on some work or something." She slipped her hand free from his, pressed it to his chest, and took her time before looking up to him. "But I'm going home to change and then go back to work, so if you'll give me the names of the other guests, I'll search out the information, print it off, and bring it back to you."

"Outstanding," Weber said, and for a second Walker had forgotten he was there.

As he placed his hand over Kate's where it was resting on his chest right before she went to pull it away, holding her there, he shook his head.

She frowned.

"If you go in," he said, "I'm going with you."

S he was sitting, or rather parked, beside Walker's desk once again. Kruso was sitting in her chair, so Kate had to turn her head to see the friendly cop as she sifted through a file or report or whatever it was. She glanced to Kate and then over to Walker, who was talking now with Medina and Weber.

"He's got a thing for you," Kruso said.

Kate wanted to roll her eyes at the detective, who said it teasingly, or so it sounded. "He just thinks he does, but he's also panicked, thinking he's just dug himself into something where he's given away all his freedom. I mean, seriously, it was as if he was pulling at his collar and couldn't breathe."

Kruso snorted. "He's got issues with letting anyone get close, but he's also not about to let you get hurt. He's put himself between you and those cops. Never seen Walker do that before. He doesn't want you involved in this case, and Walker is all about solving a case. That, my dear, is a guy who has a thing for you."

What could she say to that? Maybe it was obligation,

and she opened her mouth to say something to convince Kruso she was wrong, but nothing came out.

"Okay, let's go," Walker said. He was pulling open the drawer to his desk, taking out his keys, lifting his jacket from the back of his chair. Kate looked over to Kruso, who was ignoring both of them now.

"I need to go home and change first, grab a shower and get out of these clothes. I reek like booze, and my shirt…" She stopped talking as she glanced back at Kruso, who glanced over to her. The woman was listening.

"Fine," he said.

This time he didn't reach for her hand as she stood up, her jacket still buttoned, and slipped her purse over her shoulder. She took her time and then looked over at Walker, who was watching her again in a way that made her wonder what he was thinking. It wasn't the look of a man who was trying to get rid of her. At the same time, she didn't want to read too much into it.

He said nothing as he gestured for her to go first, and she did, marching out of the squad room, head held high, Walker right behind her.

She knew he was watching her. His gaze, she was sure, was right on her ass, so she put an extra sway in her hips and noted the desk sergeant looking up. His expression was priceless.

Walker reached around her for the door and pushed it open.

"Thank you," she said and stepped out, hearing him grunt. Whatever else he was thinking, she didn't know. Then he was beside her, walking to his car in the darkened parking lot. He opened the passenger door.

"So no backseat this time?" She couldn't resist. It was like poking a bear, from the expression on his face.

"Get in," he said. He brought his face closer to hers,

dropped his eyes to her lips, and backed up again. She had to squeeze her legs together as she touched her tongue to her lips, and then he lowered his head, and she knew he was going to kiss her. She shut her eyes, waiting for it, wanting it. Then she felt his nose by her ear.

"Get in the car now," he said, pulling away, leaving Kate wanting and speechless. His hand slid around her ass and lower to the slit in back, touching her bare leg, and she squealed, looked around, and climbed in.

He shut the door, and she watched as Walker Pruett, a cop, a man who had turned her life upside down, walked around to the driver's side, slid behind the wheel, and started the car.

CHAPTER

Sixteen

She was sexy, testing every one of Walker's boundaries. For the first time, he was thinking of what he was going to do to Kate. He wanted to put his hands on her. No, he needed to touch her, to take her, to fuck her, but she was now not a woman he could do that to. They were way past that. They'd had their night of fun, hot and sexy. Now he was twisted up in knots over the fact that she'd just given him every man's wish, letting him out of tying himself to her. He should have been happy, ecstatic, but he wasn't.

"You know you don't have to come up," she said. "This is a good time for you to just drive away. I'll shower, change, head back to work, and you can go and do whatever it is that you do, Walker."

He was parked in front of her apartment, and he knew again what she was doing. She glanced over to him, smiled, reached for the handle, and climbed out before he could say anything.

"Hold it," he said. He climbed out of the car and gave the door a shove.

"Yes?" She stopped halfway to the door, her keys now in her hand.

"Stop being a pain in the ass." He reached her side and took her keys. "This has already been decided, Kate. You're not going alone. I'm not driving off and leaving you to go and play junior detective. You'll get hurt." He jammed the keys in the lock and turned. He pulled open the door, and he could see he'd rattled her.

She stepped past him. "I'm not a pain in the ass, Walker."

He wanted to laugh as he followed her up the stairs. He still held her keys, looking for the one to unlock her door. She went to reach for them, but he held them away. Of course she rolled her eyes at him.

"Are you going to search my apartment for me, too?" she asked. "It's the green key." She pointed, and he inserted it in the deadbolt and opened her door, stepping into the apartment he'd seen only once before.

He went in first and heard the door close behind her, the lock setting. "Cleaner than I remember," he said. She wasn't much of a housekeeper, and the last time she'd had a trail of clothes on the floor. He was sure she'd stepped out of them as she walked.

She was in the kitchen, pulling open the freezer, and she held up a Lean Cuisine. "Dinner, want one?" she asked as she pulled it out of the packaging and popped it in the microwave.

"That's not real food. No," he said as she unbuttoned her coat and went to pull it off. He caught a glimpse of her bra, her breasts, the wrecked blouse. "Sorry about your shirt."

She froze and then looked over at him slowly. For a moment, he glimpsed the emotion he had seen earlier.

Then she walked out of the kitchen and into the bedroom. Her back was to him as she slipped out of her coat.

Walker moved to the doorway of her bedroom, and Kate stilled. Then she slid her hands up and slipped off her blouse. She went to reach around to unfasten her bra, but his hand was there, touching hers, stopping her. He didn't know why he did it. He stepped closer, his legs brushing hers, her ass nestled back against him. His hands were skimming her stomach and higher, covering her breasts, and he rocked with her. She rested her head back against his shoulder. He had to press a kiss to her temple, her forehead.

"Walker, you can't do this to me. We're not a couple, and I can't do the casual, no strings, no nothing." She didn't move away from him as he unfastened her bra and allowed it to fall to the floor, pulling her back against him and swaying again. He wanted her. He had to have her. He couldn't let her walk away.

But she did, even though he could feel how much she wanted him. It was something she couldn't hide. She pushed away, stepped to the bathroom, and then stopped in the doorway as she kicked off her shoes, unzipped her skirt, and allowed it to pool on the floor at her feet.

"I need a shower," she said. Then she stood there, and that was the moment when he knew he should walk away, walk out of the bedroom, and leave her be. But he couldn't as he took in that body, the woman he wanted, the woman he had to have.

"To hell with that. You're mine," he said, and he stalked toward her, his hand going to her ass, touching her, pulling her and lifting her as she wrapped her arms around his neck. He carried her into the bathroom.

CHAPTER
Seventeen

She was his. That was exactly what he'd said as he put his hands on her again, lifting her and taking her into the shower. He was behind her and inside her now as her hands pressed against the wall of the shower, holding her hips and pounding into her. She'd already screamed out his name once, but he wasn't done. Then his hands moved, touching her everywhere as if he needed to remind himself she was his. It was the possessive touch of a man putting his mark on her. It was unfamiliar, it was overwhelming, and Kate wasn't sure her legs would hold her much longer.

"Walker." Her voice caught as he squeezed her nipple between his fingers, his hand holding her breast. He pressed his teeth into her shoulder and touched with his tongue to soothe the burn from the playful bite, but he was far from gentle. No, this was a taking, a shagging, far different from before. Then he slowed, and she felt him, larger, thicker. He swore. He had a condom on, protection, and she was grateful for that even though she'd have loved to feel all his warmth as he came inside her again and again.

"Fuck, oh my good God, Kate, you're so sweet." He held himself against her, and she couldn't move. The water was pouring down on them. It was still warm, but she wondered how much longer it would last until it went cold.

He pressed a kiss to her ear, and she just leaned against the tile as he pulled out and reached around to turn the water off.

She shut her eyes and shivered at the loss of his body, his warmth, when he stepped away.

"Hey, come on out, dry off." He pulled open the curtain, reached for a towel, and wrapped it around her first. When she looked up at Walker, he was watching her with an expression on his face that was so tender. Why wasn't he freaking out, looking to leave? "You look worried or something. What is it?" he asked as he grabbed a second towel from the cupboard in her bathroom. It wasn't lost on her how small her bathroom was with the likes of Walker Pruett invading it. The fact was that he seemed to be far more comfortable here than she'd expected. It unsettled her.

"What is this, Walker? I can't do the sex and no strings thing. I already gave you your out, saving you from yourself. Remember, we're not girlfriend and boyfriend. You can't handle it, and I can't be sitting here again, waiting for you to call, wondering if you're thinking of me or if you've already moved on and picked up some other woman to screw, maybe even forgotten my name. I was wrong for being easy the first time, for letting you screw me the way you did, but, Walker, I swear, the way you touch me, look at me, I can't say no, so please don't take advantage of me. Don't hurt me." There, she'd said it. Good girl—or not.

He frowned, and she didn't have a clue what he was thinking. "You're mine. Did I not just make that perfectly clear?" he said, his voice not soft or tender. It was rough, and there was nothing indecisive or wimpy there, but then, Walker never did anything unless he meant it. He knew what he wanted. He did what he wanted. Even when he took her, he made sure she understood very clearly who was inside her, who was fucking her. He was a man with an energy that took over a room, took over her. Maybe it was the thought of belonging to Walker Pruett that had her warming again, had her trembling and wanting to feel him put his mark all over her. She had to stop, look away.

"But I told you I'm not holding you to what you said." Her voice sounded so odd, breathless.

He shook his head, wrapping the towel around his waist and stepping toward her. He put his fingers on the towel tucked against her breasts. Her hair was wet, and she brushed it back from her face. "Well, maybe I want to be held to what I said. Did you think of that?"

She wondered for a moment whether he really meant it. "Walker…"

He tilted his head, his expression sure, and that part puzzled her.

She hesitated, licked her lip, and he wasn't running or reaching for the door or leaving. "Okay," she said, and she stood on her tiptoes, pressing her lips to his, allowing the towel to drop to the floor.

CHAPTER
Eighteen

She was wearing blue jeans and a simple T-shirt over a black lace bra. It wasn't lost on him that she'd omitted underwear. Her hair was still damp, and she had a healthy glow on her cheeks from where he'd fucked her—no, loved her again, on the bed this time, slowly and tenderly, taking his time and watching her for every reaction, every response she had to him.

The woman was so damn responsive. Her eyes, her body, her skin…she couldn't hide anything from him, and she tasted better than the sweetest dessert. She was under his skin and inside him, and he was in new territory. Never in all his years had he ever been faithful to one woman, had one woman, called a woman his.

It was after midnight, and he walked through the front door of the hotel with Kate's hand in his. The bar was still open, the restaurant closed, and he noted a janitor cleaning the floor by the elevator.

"Let's go in the back office," she said, and he took in the front desk, where there was no one around. "That's odd."

"What is?" He was looking around at the browns and golds, the empty sofas, the dim dining room, which had closed up for the night.

"Jamie isn't there." She tilted her head and walked around the front desk. Walker followed her to the office behind it. The door was open a crack, and a light was on, but no one was there. "Maybe he went to the washroom," she said.

Walker took in the office. It wasn't square, longer on one side with a desk built against the entire wall. Two office chairs were pushed in, and it was spotless. Papers were stacked neatly at one far corner, and plastic organizers stuffed with paper lined the wall.

Kate turned on the computer.

"What are you doing?" he asked as she pulled out one of the chairs and sat down as the computer screen turned on. She was typing on the keyboard, pulling up something on the screen.

"Give me the names, and I'll pull up those guests' folios and print off the details. Seeing it always helps jog my memory." She glanced over to the door and then up to Walker. "Let me know if you hear someone coming."

She smiled, and he couldn't help himself from leaning down and kissing those lips. They were full, pink, a little swollen from how he'd taken her, kissed her, and loved her earlier that night. She had to know now who she belonged to. He had to stop his head from going down that road, thinking of her heat, because she was distracting him, and right now he couldn't afford to be off his game.

He pulled his notebook from his jacket pocket and opened to a page where he'd listed names. "Those five," he said. "The dates are approximate." He tapped the paper, went to the door, and looked out. He noticed a tall, lanky young man with dark hair, wearing the same uniform Kate had, a dark sports coat and a name tag.

"There's a guy coming, dark hair, young man. Kate," he prompted. He heard her jump up and step around him. If they were anywhere else, he would have stopped her or moved her behind him, but this was her work, her people, her career, and him being here with her was putting her job in jeopardy.

"Kate, what are you doing here?" The young man appeared startled as he strode around the front desk, opened a drawer, stuck a key inside, and closed it again.

"Had to check on something. Just following up on a complaint earlier and checking on room inventory. Oh, and this is my boyfriend," she added. She glanced back, leaned casually toward Walker. "Walker, this is Jamie. Jamie, Walker." She gestured between them.

The young man was wearing a wedding ring but appeared fresh out of high school. Walker wondered how old he was.

"Hey, pleasure." The kid stuck out his hand. Walker shook it, and it was strong, but Jamie pulled away and flashed a bright, mischievous smile at Kate.

"Was wondering where you were when we came in," she said. "No one was there."

Jamie just shrugged, typing something in the computer. "Just making sure things are locked up: the exercise room, the back door, the stairwell. Making sure everything's all quiet and nothing unusual's going on."

"Isn't security supposed to do that?" Kate asked.

Walker noticed she was frowning, and this time he noted Jamie's expression. It wasn't the look of someone about to explain himself. For a minute, he was sure this kid thought he could do anything he wanted. He didn't see Kate as his boss. He wondered if she knew.

"Most times I do a follow-up. Found a door open once in the back stairwell at night. Doesn't hurt to do it twice. So why are you here again?"

The kid was sharp, and Walker was wondering as he looked around. Not much staff on this time of night, but then, there wouldn't be.

"Kate, you finish up and then we'll get going," he said, which got her attention. Maybe she understood his meaning, as she nodded. He could tell something was bothering her by her expression, though.

"Sure. I'll just be another minute." She tapped the counter and moved into the back room.

Jamie glanced around, and for a minute Walker wondered if he was going to follow Kate. Curiosity wasn't such a good thing. "So, Jamie, how long have you worked here?" He stepped around the counter so Jamie had to turn, the office now at his back.

"About a year," he said. "Go to school during the day."

"That's quite a load. When do you sleep?" He knew of people who'd done this, friends he'd had, and many had been so exhausted they'd struggled through school. Many had popped pills, too. He took in the kid's wedding ring, a simple gold band.

"I manage to get by. Grab a few hours when it's slow."

He noticed Kate in the back office, moving around, lifting papers from a printer. She glanced over her shoulder at him and mouthed, *Got it.*

Then she appeared by his side, her coat over her arm, her big baggy purse looped over her shoulder. "Any problems tonight?" she said to Jamie.

"No, all quiet." He shook his head, leaned down on the counter, and flashed a smile to Kate and then Walker.

All Walker could think as he shook his head was *Young and foolish.*

S he was walking beside Walker. His arm was brushing hers, and her heart was racing, not only because she was still trying to get her head around the fact that Walker was here and that he wanted her, and his hand now was settled possessively on her lower back as they strode out of the hotel, but because she felt she'd just done something sneaky for the first time.

Walker leaned down and opened the passenger door, holding the frame, resting his hand on her shoulder as she glanced back to the hotel, seeing Jamie behind the front desk, looking down at the computer. She'd never stopped in at night when he was working, so she was surprised to know he was leaving the desk unattended as he was. It was just something she never did unless she had to go to the bathroom.

"What's wrong?" Walker turned his head to look where she was.

She just shook her head as she looked up to him. Even though it was dark out, she knew the man cared for her. She could see how he was here with her and not seeming as if he needed to get away. That was the kind of look she was familiar with. Maybe that was why she was so unsettled.

"Get in," he said.

He closed the door after she had settled in the passenger seat, and she pulled out the folios of the guests he'd listed. He slid behind the wheel and shoved the keys in the ignition as she unfolded the papers.

"All these guests were here on business," she said. "As you can see in the notes, it lists their companies. They weren't here long, only a few nights each. I remember them, but then, I do most guests. There aren't that many who become forgettable." She lowered the papers as she looked over to her guy, who had tossed his hand over the back of the seat, touching her shoulder.

"Any of these guys do anything or go anywhere that you can remember?"

She sifted through the names again: Clark, Selkirk, Anderson, Martin, and Shawnessy. Then she remembered and saw her note on the bottom, *FR*. She smiled to herself.

"What?" Walker asked.

"This guy, Jim Anderson, I remember him. He's from Edmonton, Alberta, up in Canada. He was meeting with a bunch of sales reps from a food distributor down here, a guys' weekend away, and he was waiting in the lobby. Had chatted with me for a bit, and then he said something to a lady waiting over on a sofa in the lobby. There was a woman dressed sharply, in a skirt and jacket, sitting on a sofa. She'd been waiting for a dinner date to join her, and they were going into the restaurant. He apparently thought she was some call girl he ordered. The lady was livid, told him to get lost, and he hurried away. I asked her when he left, seeing how mad and upset she was, if everything was all right, and she told me he asked if she was the lady he'd ordered. She was mortified. I felt bad for her."

"Well, what did you do?" Walker ran his finger over his lips.

"Nothing. I told Keith that we had some guest trying to bring hookers into the hotel. Gave him his name, told him what happened. He said not to worry about it, he'd handle it."

"Did he?"

"I don't know, but I always put these initials on the bottom of a folio on the computer just for my reference. FR, see?" She gestured to her notes under the comments section. "Stands for 'fucker' so I know the guy's a two timer. Not that it happens often, but when it does, those guys stand out. You see them walk back into the hotel with a woman up to their room, or housekeeping reports they had one stay over. All of these guys can't even be bothered to take off their wedding rings. Men…sometimes I wonder how stupid they can be." She noticed the way Walker winced.

"Well, at least not all guys are like that, Kate," he said. "So does your hotel promote that kind of thing, maybe offer something illegal on the side, escort service or something?"

"We're a reputable hotel, Walker. I wouldn't be working here if there was anything going on like that. There are enough hotels and motels in the city that offer that kind of service. We're not one of them," she added, wondering now exactly what Keith had done with Mr. Anderson. Maybe nothing, but then, nothing else had been reported after that.

"And these other guys on the list?" Walker's cell phone rang, and he pulled it from his pocket. "Hold that thought." He glanced at the screen. "Walker here," he said, and he reached for the papers Kate was holding. "You did what? What did it show? Seriously, a woman?"

She could hear a man's voice on the other end.

"Any ID on who it is?" He pinched the bridge of his nose. "We're outside the hotel now. Kate just pulled up the names, printed off the information. As I recall, each of these guys wasn't all that forthcoming. One of them may have been arranging for a hooker." Then he was nodding. "Text me the photo."

She sat there as Walker hung up, then glanced out the window and back to her. "This isn't what I thought. Weber got a hold of the surveillance. It was a woman who came out of the alley, so at least we have a place to start." His phone beeped, and he stared at the screen, shaking his head, and then tossed the phone on the seat between them. "Put your seatbelt on," he said as he started the car.

As Kate lifted the phone and took in the image of Carl Eastman with a short dark-haired woman behind him, she zoomed in—because that woman, the young lady, she knew she'd seen her before.

"I know her!" she said. "I mean, I don't know her, but that's Jamie's wife." She looked over to Walker, then pulled open the door and stepped out of the car.

———

Before he could get his head around the fact that Kate had just ID'ed the suspect, she was pressing open the door to the hotel and heading right for the front desk, and she was mad.

Walker turned off the car and raced after her. "Kate," he called out. He grabbed his phone, dialed, and pressed it to his ear.

"Thought you were on your way back here," Weber said.

"That photo you just sent, Kate said it's the wife of the front desk clerk on duty right now," Walker said into the phone as he raced after Kate, who was already at the desk, already speaking with Jamie—not speaking, yelling. "Get down here now," he snapped before hanging up.

By the time Walker had reached the desk, Jamie's face had paled, and he had gone to race out of the hotel, but Kate had gotten in his way. She grabbed his arm, and he knocked her down, but Walker tackled him and drove his fist into his face, then rolled him over onto his stomach, pulling his hands behind his back.

"Kate, are you okay?" he called out. He glanced to where she was on her hands and knees, and she sat up, brushing off her jeans.

"Fine," she said. "I can't believe it. Jamie, what did you do? That was your wife behind a guest. She killed him! Are you part of this?" Kate was standing over him as Walker slapped metal cuffs on his wrists.

Walker grabbed Jamie's jacket from between his shoulders and helped him up, and Jamie shook his head, standing there, staring at Kate and then Walker. The kid was shaking, but his lips were tight as if he had no intention of talking.

"I want a lawyer. I'm not saying anything until I get a lawyer."

Walker heard the car, and Weber and Medina both hurried in.

"You can have a lawyer, but you're also going to tell us where your wife is," Walker said as the other two detectives joined him.

Kate turned, heading over to the front desk and into the office in back. For the life of him, he didn't know what she was doing, but when she came back out with a sticky note with an address scribbled on it, she handed it to Weber. "This is Jamie's home address, where his wife will be." His Kate, appearing now as if she alone was responsible for solving the crime, turned to him and said, "I need to call Keith, let him know what's happened." She touched Walker's arm.

For the first time, as Walker listened to Medina read Jamie his rights, effectively taking over what once had been his case, and to his girlfriend talking on the phone, handling this hotel situation, her back to him, Walker realized in an odd way that he was the one who was waiting now.

Twenty

I t was three in the morning when Walker locked the
door.

The lights were off, the house was quiet, and Kate was
asleep upstairs. It had been quite a night, since he now had
a girl—an official girlfriend, as he had told everyone—had
solved a case in a way he'd never expected, and was no
longer freaking out at the thought of not being a
single man.

Kate was a woman who held his interest, drove him
crazy, and had gotten inside him as no one had before. He
wanted to protect her, keep her close, and hurt anyone who
tried to mess with her. Maybe it had taken him this long to
understand the feelings he actually had for her, because
what he felt for Kate didn't terrify him as he'd thought it
would, believed it would. Standing behind her, letting any
and every man know who she was to him, changed the
dynamics considerably in how people spoke to her and
treated her.

Even her boss, Keith, who had raced into the hotel to
learn that Jamie and his wife had been scoping out the

guests, had changed his attitude of trying to grind Kate down after taking a second and third look over to Walker, knowing that he could no longer treat her the way he had.

He wondered whether Kate knew. Maybe she did, maybe she didn't, but it wasn't something he was going to point out.

Jamie and his wife had been responsible for the robberies, and Jamie's wife had panicked when Carl Eastman had fought her, so she'd hit him across the head, knocking him down. She'd never meant to kill him, Walker had been told. It had just happened, all because the couple were young and strapped financially, with student loans, a pile of debt, and not enough money to pay the rent. Jamie had started out by robbing businessmen in town for the few hundreds they had in cash in their wallets, and he had been arranging call girls for businessmen who hinted at that need. He'd taken a fee like a pimp, and Walker was still trying to understand how no one in management—Keith, Tony, or anyone in security—had caught on to what he had been doing.

Kate, though, was unsettled. She had a lot to think about, a lot to understand, because tonight she was upstairs in Walker's bed, waiting for him to join her and pull her into his arms, and tomorrow would be soon enough for them to start making plans for a future together. Now he finally understood what people said, what men said about knowing when they met the one. There was one thing about men, they always had a plan, and Walker's plan now was all about him and Kate.

Chapter 21

Kate was in his bed, sharing his one and only pillow. There was something about Walker Pruett as she watched him sleep, his arm resting across his forehead. Some of the hard edge of his expression had softened a bit, and she was tempted to reach over and touch his face, to kiss him, to feel him as he slowly woke. It would be a first, so intimate, but was he really ready? And, more importantly, was she?

Even though they had the best sex, they had never spent the night together, sleeping together, side to side, face to face. Waking together in the morning, in the light of day, was an intimacy meant to be shared with someone Kate truly cared for, never something she did when she was just screwing around with someone. No, when she was keeping it light and commitment free, she never broke that cardinal rule and stayed over. Yet here she was in Walker's bed because he'd said she was now his girl. She did want that, but the doubts about how long he'd last until he began to feel cornered wouldn't stop dogging her.

But then, this was where a relationship started, and

now Kate had to wonder if in fact, despite all Walker's panic and running, maybe she was the one who wasn't ready now. Was this what she wanted, this something with Walker? She'd fought so hard with the dating scene, looking for Mr. Right, and here he was.

She breathed in, lying on her side, rubbing her legs together. Yeah, she did want him, and she wanted him to want her. It wasn't so much that they were *together* together, because she still had her apartment, and this was Walker's house, his place. It was a very clear division, because that ultimate commitment, merging everything, was something neither of them would be able to do quite yet. This was supposed to be an exciting time, a fun time of getting to know each other.

The problem was, and Kate supposed this was where her doubts were stemming from, that Walker had decided he was no longer single and they were now together. She'd been happy with that to a point, and she was more at ease about whatever would come out of it down the road now that she had a little more of a guarantee that she was no longer alone, so why was she still on edge?

His eyes were now open, and he took a breath, slowly turning as he stretched. The green of his eyes, so soft and vivid, had her stomach taking a leap. She'd never seen them in this light, not fresh from sleep when he was vulnerable and hadn't had the chance to hammer up all the walls he built whenever his conscious brain took over.

"Mmm, how long've you been awake? What time is it?" He didn't wait for her to respond as he rolled to his side and looked at his watch. She could see him change as he pulled away from her and sat at the edge of the bed. "Can't believe how late it is. Half the morning's gone." He was scrubbing his face with both hands, and all Kate could do was stare at his naked back. It was strong and perfectly sculpted, although there was a scar in the middle just above his waist, a faint white line of puckered skin.

Kate couldn't help reaching out and touching it, skimming it with her finger. "What happened here?"

He reacted to her touch, reaching around, taking her hand. The sheet over his waist fell away as he turned and slipped his hand over her stomach, covering one of her breasts. She wasn't a fool; she knew the man favored them.

"Shot. It was stupid, my younger days as a newbie cop," he said as he slid up over her, skin to skin, settling between her legs. He pressed a kiss to her lips, his hands sliding to her hips and pulling her up. "Let's go shower," he said. "You can wash my back, and then I have to go down to the precinct. What about you? What are you doing today?"

It sounded so normal, maybe something couples did, but Walker was far from the easy, committed type of guy who put his girl first, let alone did the domestic talk, the *How was your day?* kind of thing. Maybe Kate made a face or winced.

"What?" he said. His expression was priceless.

"You're taking this girlfriend/boyfriend 'Let's share everything about our day' thing a little over the top, Walker. Seriously, don't ask because you think you should. You're all about you. I'm a big girl and knew that from the get-go, and now…"

His lips were on hers, effectively shutting her up. He pulled her against him, standing, backing her to the bedroom wall. His hands were on her ass, about to lift her as he pulled away, and of course she was now putty in his hands. She shook her head, resting her hands on his chest before he kissed her again. "Walker…"

He lifted her, and her legs went around him as if they had a mind of their own. They knew exactly what he was about and how much she enjoyed what he did to her. Now he had her back on the bed and was doing the most delicious erotic things to her, the way his hands moved over her, taking her breasts and touching, caressing, as if not a part of her body wasn't his. Then he was covering himself again from the box of condoms he'd yanked from the bedside drawer.

He pushed her legs up and open and slid inside her again. It was the way he moved, the way he held her legs just below her knees so she couldn't pull away, move away, with each thrust inside her. He took in her expression, the squeak escaping from her throat, as she'd now lost any ability to speak at all. That was something only Walker could do to her.

His expression as he moved inside her harder, faster, holding her so she couldn't move, was so alpha male, so cop. He was a man who was all about himself, his needs, his wants, his control. Maybe that was why she liked this so much.

She couldn't hold herself back. She felt the current breaking apart inside her. Of course, in that moment, from the sly grin, she knew he felt it. He knew he could bend her to his will, knowing she was close to the edge because he was the one bringing her there.

"Come on, Kate. Get there," he growled at her as he moved faster, harder. She screamed and tried to move but couldn't from wave after wave of ecstasy that he rocked from her. He was holding her so hard, and she heard him and felt him vividly as if their worlds had collided. At the same time, everything outside could have come to a standstill and she wouldn't have cared or heard or even wondered. Walker moved inside her one last time, her legs looped over his arms as he leaned across her, pinning her down. She ran her hands over his back, breathing as hard as he was at the unexpected sexual romp that was over as fast as it had begun, but it had been completely satisfying, and, as always, because this was Walker, completely off the charts. She patted his back again, as her legs were beginning to cramp from being spread so wide.

"You can drop me off at home on your way," she said. She smoothed her hand over his shoulders as he pulled out. When he stepped back, her legs fell like limp noodles over the edge of the bed as she stayed where she was. Walker, though, appeared rattled as he tore off his condom and stepped into the bathroom. She could hear him tossing it into the garbage. Kate sat up, taking in the mess of condom packages, the box on the floor, the packets on the bed.

She heard the shower, so she slipped off the bed and followed him into the bathroom, where he was now stepping into the tub and pulling the curtain closed. She lifted the curtain back and stepped in behind him, but he only glanced her way. She wondered where the chatty Walker had gone.

"I need to be at work for the late afternoon shift," she said, "but I'm going to go in earlier to see Tony about last night. I'm sure a lot of cleanup needs to be done. Come to think about it, I should check my phone. I thought I'd have been called in. I'm sure the owner's been contacted, and since I was responsible for uncovering the robbery…"

Walker moved over, pulling Kate beside him under the spray. She tilted her head back in the hot water, which felt so good.

"You identified Jamie's wife from the screenshot of the video," Walker said as he scrubbed his short hair with shampoo before grabbing a bar of soap, lathering it up, and running it over his body. He handed it to her as he rinsed off, and she soaped herself, taking in this complex man, wondering what he was up to now.

"You know I helped," she said. "If it wasn't for me, your case would still be wide open, so why do you have such a hard time saying I was responsible for closing it?" She squirted shampoo into her palm and took in the brand, a cheap department store kind she'd never use. She rinsed the shampoo from her hand down the drain. She'd wash her hair at home.

"Kate, you're an amateur, and I didn't want you involved at all, if you recall. Things with you can go very badly very quickly. Look what you did last night, racing in to confront Jamie, and you got yourself knocked down. You could have been hurt or worse. You're not a cop." He reached around her and turned off the water, and she couldn't believe how he was turning this around on her as if he couldn't see how much she'd contributed.

He stepped out of the tub and reached for a towel, then ran it over his head and his chest. Kate stepped out, and Walker handed her a deep red one from the rack. She dried the ends of her hair as Walker hung his towel back on the rack, standing there with his hand on his hips, so comfortable naked in the light of day. He didn't have a shy bone in his body, but looking at him and how spectacular he was, the man had a right to be so confident. He was staring at her as if he were fully clothed, and she was very aware then that Walker would never be a man she could bend to her will. He was so strong minded that butting heads with him was enjoyable and a rather fun pastime. He would definitely keep her on her toes.

"Maybe so, Walker, but without my help last night you'd still be sitting at square one, trying to figure out who did it. As I'll remind you again, I'm the one who saw the photo of Jamie's wife, Tess, on the surveillance and told you who she was. You may have eventually figured it out, but at what cost? How many others would have been robbed, killed?"

There, damn, she was proud of herself, and the expression on Walker's face and the way he nearly snarled back at her with a loss of a comeback had her wanting to dance naked all the way back to the bedroom.

Chapter 22

He had done it again, dropped her off at her door, although this time he had kissed her before she stepped out of his car wearing last night's clothes, a T-shirt and blue jeans. Even though she had showered, she still felt grungy. Walker, being Walker, pulled away as soon as she'd opened the door, not slowly like a normal person but zipping into traffic as if he couldn't get away fast enough. Some things, she supposed, would never change.

But then, it wasn't as if she was surprised. She'd seen it with Walker. The moment he had been getting dressed, he was already thinking, distracted. She supposed his head was already tackling every case or whatever it was he needed to do today. The man could go from zero to six hundred in a few seconds flat. He was far from boring, average, a challenge she wondered whether she was ready for.

She showered again, this time using her favorite salon shampoo and drying her hair so it fell in soft waves past her shoulders. She applied powder, blush, and mascara and pulled on clean dark pants, a short-sleeved white blouse with ruffles, and her dark blazer, her nametag still fastened on the left above her breast. She took one last look at her image in the mirror before reaching for her black and white coat and slipping it on, then heading out the door and walking the few blocks to work. She couldn't keep the bounce from her step as she walked in her black flats, her coat undone. Today the sun had decided to shine.

It matched her mood, and she didn't think anything today could bring her down. No, the sun was out, the stars had aligned, she had a boyfriend, and Jamie had been caught. All was perfect. So was the easy smile that touched her lips as she pulled open the front door of the Hotel Monaco and strode to the front desk, but as she took in her bosses, both of them, Keith and Tony, watching her from behind the front desk, something screamed at her to be careful. Neither of them appeared happy.

She could feel the edge about them as she stepped closer, a hardness that appeared on Tony's face and something in Keith's expression that made a knot tighten in the pit of her stomach. She didn't have a chance to say a word, or maybe she was trying to get her tongue to move, when Tony stepped from behind the desk as if to block her and gestured to the stairs.

"Kate, I'd like a word." It was cold and impersonal, a way he'd never spoken to her before.

She swallowed. "Sure," she said. Again she swallowed the lump in her throat. Her hands were now shaking, so she fisted them and followed Tony, glancing back once to Keith, who didn't even look her way. He was at the desk, working a shift, which was something he never did. Okay, this wasn't good.

She wanted to say something to Tony that would break the ice, lighten the mood a bit, but for the life of her she couldn't figure out what. "So…"

"Not here," he said, cutting her off before she could even finish. His tone was sharp, something she'd never experienced from Tony but had seen a time or two when he had it in for someone else.

His office was downstairs on the lower level with the accounting department. It was unusually quiet this afternoon as she followed him inside. It was cold, and the energy had her pulling her lower lip between her teeth. She hesitated only a second before taking a seat, perching on the edge of the chair, too uncomfortable to sit back. Tony undid his suit jacket button and sat in his chair behind his desk. A whoosh in the leather sounded as he pulled it forward, but he still hadn't looked across to her.

Oh, this wasn't good.

He rested both arms on the desk before looking over to her. Yup, she was in trouble.

She swallowed.

"I'm trying to understand something, Kate, and I'm hoping you can enlighten me."

"Sure." She swallowed again, her foot now shaking, tapping the ground so she had to press her hand to her knee to get it to stop.

"You brought the police into this hotel without consulting with your supervisor. You logged on to the computer and tapped in to guest information, then printed it off and gave it to an outside person—confidential information—after I had specifically told one cop not to come back without a warrant. Yet you decided you could make all the decisions here and hand over anything you wanted. You're a nobody, Kate, just a junior front desk assistant with no power to piss in any pot."

He was staring at her hard, his hand gesturing softly. She wasn't a fool. She knew there was nothing soft or considerate about his approach, and the way he was talking to her was dashing her hopes of coming out of this unscathed. At the same time, she was trying to understand —no, get her head around the fact that he knew she'd printed off those folios. How? She hadn't even told Keith last night that she'd given those to Walker, and she was pretty sure he had passed them on to those two cops who were investigating the murder of poor Mr. Eastman.

Tony's face was tight, hard, and unsmiling.

"Yes, but I'm not sure I understand why you're upset with me. Jamie was robbing people. His wife killed one of the guests who was staying at this hotel. I can't see how me—"

"That's irrelevant, Kate. The fact that you used your position here to come in and take documents, access confidential, protected guest information, and give that to anyone is a fireable offense."

She was positive she wasn't hearing correctly. Of course she'd misunderstood. She was the hero. In fact, she'd stopped a crime that had been happening right under management's noses. They should have been thanking her. This was all wrong.

"Ah, listen, Tony, maybe you're misunderstanding…"

"No, I think not, Kate. In fact, I've learned that the cop I asked not to return until he had a search warrant, only for him to come back with you, is your boyfriend." Tony was shaking his head, and he leaned forward, jabbing his finger to the door. "No, Kate, whatever Jamie did is irrelevant. What you did was a betrayal of trust."

There was a knock on the open door. She glanced up to see Keith standing there, looking over to Tony.

"You tell her?" Keith asked, but he only glanced quickly at Kate. His expression was tired, unfriendly, hard, and for a moment it seemed different from last night. She couldn't make sense of it.

"Was about to. Kate, you are dismissed. Turn in your badge and keys with Keith. If you have any personal belongings here, they'll be sent to you along with your last check."

This was worse that she suspected. Her legs were shaking, her insides trembling as she reached into her purse and pulled out her keys. The key to the front desk office and administration was on the same key ring as her house keys. Her hands were sweating, and she couldn't get the ring apart with her fingers.

"Here." Keith reached for her keys.

"Those two." She pointed, and for a moment she sensed something from him that resembled sympathy, but that couldn't be, because he didn't have compassion—not for her, at least. She couldn't look at him as he removed the keys and handed her keychain back.

"Let's go," he said, gesturing to the open door after taking a step back.

"Escort her off the property—and, Kate, don't return, because security will be alerted. You're not to set foot back on the premises for any reason. Do not patronize the restaurant or bar. You won't be served."

She glanced back at Tony, who was now standing. The two keys Keith had removed from the keychain were sitting at the edge of the desk. She hadn't seen him set them down, and then she remembered her ID badge and removed it from her jacket pocket. The blazer was also part of the staff uniform. She wondered whether he'd want that back, too.

She didn't think as she took off her coat and slipped off the blazer with her name-tag still pinned on it, then dumped it on the chair and turned to walk out the door, pulling on her jacket. Keith followed, leading her to a side door that led out to the alley, where she stepped out.

"Kate," he said before she could take another step. "Look, if it's worth anything to you, I'm sorry. What Jamie did was bad. Seems you've been caught in the fallout. It was just bad timing, that cop showing up this morning to talk to Tony and wrapping up those loose ends. You really accessed guest information and gave it to the police?" He shook his head, holding the door as if considering. "Ballsy, Kate. Stupid, but good for you. Take care."

As he closed the door, Kate shut her eyes for a second. It was sinking in that someone had just hung her out to dry, and she had a pretty good idea who that someone was.

Chapter 23

Weber was just coming out of the captain's office as Walker slid off his jacket and set it around the back of his chair. He glanced over to Kruso, whose red hair was sticking up at the back as if she'd gone to bed with it wet. Her nose was stuck in a file, reading.

"How's your girlfriend?" She didn't even look up as she turned a page, resting her chin on her hand.

"Kate's fine." It was so new, having anyone ask and point out who Kate was to him. Of course it felt weird, but he realized he didn't have that choking feeling that made him want to reach up and pull at his collar. No, there was an odd sense of amusement at having Kate, her spunk, her attitude, her fire, everything about her, belong to him. He realized Kruso was watching him with a smug expression. "What?" he added. It was damn uncomfortable having the spotlight on him as it was now.

She licked her finger as she turned a page over in the file on her desk. Her gaze never left Walker. "Nothing, just glad to see you finally figured out what was in front of you all along, is all. You took long enough."

"There you are," Weber said before Walker could reply. He was a cocky bastard at times, and he strode up to Walker's desk, then glanced once at Kruso before gesturing to the captain's office. "Just wanted to give you a heads-up that Jamie Bishop is out. The wife, Tess, made bail, too."

For the life of him, Walker didn't know how that was possible. He looked to Kruso, who appeared as thrown as he was. "How would a cash-strapped couple make bail?"

"Seems the general manager of the Hotel Monaco sent down his lawyer, a good one. They're working out a plea deal with the district attorney for voluntary manslaughter."

"Are you kidding, for bashing a man over the head not once but repeatedly? There's no way."

Weber was shaking his head. "Out of my hands. The DA is making the call on this but hasn't decided yet. That's why Medina and I went down and paid a visit to that GM, Tony Drummond. Would have expected more cooperation, considering one of his employees was targeting guests. The publicity alone could damage the hotel's reputation."

"You insinuated that little threat to Mr. Drummond?" Walker said, though he didn't say it like a question, as he already knew Weber had done just that. He'd have done the same.

Weber shrugged. "Of course. After showing him the folios your girlfriend printed off of the other guests, though, he became completely uncooperative and advised that all further communication had to be done through his lawyer."

Walker wasn't sure he'd heard correctly, but he knew he had when he glanced over to see alarm on Kruso's face. "You didn't by any chance tell him Kate had printed those off?"

Weber shuffled his feet, but at the same time he was

shaking his head. "Your girlfriend did the right thing, accessing that information."

"So that's a yes, you asshole," Walker said. "Unbelievable. You have any idea what you just did, you stupid prick? You could cause problems for Kate at work." He reached for his phone and pressed Kate's saved number. The least he could do was give her a heads-up. He stared at the picture he'd taken of her while she'd been sleeping. That was for him only. She was so vulnerable then. He wondered whether she knew that.

"You're being dramatic," Weber said. "Besides, I needed to shake that guy up. I have a hard time believing a manager didn't know what all his staff were doing or what was going on in his hotel. I can't help wondering if maybe there's more we're missing, which brings me to another matter. We'd like to speak with Kate again, get her read on this manager, more on the hotel. Maybe there's more she can dig around and get…"

He heard the chair squeak. By the time he looked up, Kruso was out of her chair, a hand to Weber's chest, standing so Walker would have to move her to get at Weber. She had to know Weber was pushing way past what was okay. Every one of Walker's protective instincts was just itching to shove Weber out of there.

"Just so you understand," Walker said, "and let me make this clear to you in case there's any misunderstanding and you can't quite get it through that thick head of yours, you're fucking with what's mine. You fucking with Kate's career, making things a little harder for her, is the same as messing with me. I'm sure you understand exactly what I'm getting at, so stop. Whatever you do, you'd better hope and pray that nothing will impact Kate in any way." He jabbed his finger, feeling very much in control as he watched Weber roll his eyes, step around Kruso, and leave.

His call went to voicemail then. "Kate, Walker here. Listen, give me a call when you get a minute. I need to talk to you about something that's come up." He slipped his phone onto his desk and took in Kruso, who didn't say a word as she slid back into her chair.

She looked up at him again as he stared at the phone, thinking. "No luck?" she finally said.

He shook his head, but then, when she was at work she couldn't really answer her cell phone. He picked up his phone again to call the hotel.

"What are you doing?" Kruso asked.

"Calling Kate at work." He found the number for the hotel and started to dial. "What?" he said when he took in Kruso's expression.

"Nothing, just amazed, is all, since it was just yesterday that the thought of having a girlfriend would have sent you running. Now look, you needing to keep tabs, touch base…"

"Hotel Monaco." The phone was answered by a deep male voice.

"Kate Sikes, please," Walker said.

There was a pause before the man said, "I'm sorry, sir. Kate no longer works here. Is there something I can help you with?"

"Ah, no," he said before hanging up, now sure that Weber's little meeting with the GM would have more consequences than he'd expected.

Chapter 24

Kate stared into the container of chocolate fudge ice cream, which was over half gone. Maybe that accounted for the sick feeling in the pit of her stomach. She vaguely remembered the trip to the grocery store on the way home, which had been done in a haze after the humiliating way she'd been walked out. It was horrible, being fired, and she didn't think her insides had stopped trembling from the moment Tony had turned those hate-filled eyes on her.

She couldn't remember anyone ever looking at her as if she'd betrayed him. It was horrible, being seen as such a vile, despicable person when she'd been the one to expose Jamie and his wife—or partly, anyway.

Then, of course, she couldn't help reliving every word and moment of the horrible meeting over and over as she dug into the rich chocolate ice cream, unable to taste all that creamy sweetness as she shoveled it down. It wasn't so much that she loved chocolate but that mountain blue-berry, the flavor she normally went for, was sold out. How cruel, since it was the only flavor that could have picked up her mood. The chocolatey fudge had been what she'd settled on while struggling to hold back the tears until she made it home and shut the door to her apartment, therefore locking out the world.

She sat on her sofa, the one with the plush cushions of red and brown, a blanket over her, her face itchy from the tears she'd cried, and watched her cell phone screen light up with Walker's number on the sofa table. It flashed once, and she ignored it. At any other time, of course, she'd have leaped for the phone, but after today, this shitty day, she didn't feel much like talking to anyone. Then her mom called, and again she let it go to voicemail, because otherwise she too would know.

No, she planned to just hole up here and lick her wounds and hide from everyone until…? She no idea.

Then her cell phone was ringing again. Walker's number flashed on the screen. Maybe he knew, but she couldn't make herself reach forward and pick up the phone to answer it. She just stared at it until it stopped ringing. Then there was a pounding on the door. She jumped.

"Kate!"

Oh, crap, it was Walker. Maybe if she said nothing and didn't make a sound, he'd go away. Then she heard a key in the lock, him talking to someone, and then footsteps. She had to look a sight, and at the same time she was horrified he could just walk in. She didn't move from where she was hunkered down, and she had to look up as he stood behind the sofa where she sat huddled with her tub of ice cream, the spoon still sticking up. Her skin felt so tight and raw from crying, and a pile of used tissues lay all around her from wiping her tears away and blowing her nose over and over.

Walker just stood there, his face grim, his hands shoved

in his leather jacket pockets. It was a look she was sure she'd have loved at any other time, but right now she was having a hard time absorbing everything that had happened: her and Walker, the mess at work, and now, most of all, how she was unemployed, fired from an industry that was far from forgiving and tended to share everything about employees and management throughout the area—the reputable ones, anyway. She was so screwed.

"What happened? Did you get my message?" Walker asked. "Why didn't you answer the door? You ignoring me?" He wasn't giving her a chance to answer, and the only thing she could do was shrug, because when she went to speak, her voice caught.

He must have known, as he walked around the sofa and took in the mess, the box of Kleenex beside her and the tub of ice cream, which he lifted from her lap and moved to the coffee table. He winced. There was her answer to how bad she looked.

"What happened?" he asked again.

"I got fired." Her voice was scratchy, and of course she couldn't hide the fact that she'd been bawling like a baby. Guys hated that. Now she wanted to cry again. Just thinking of what had happened and seeing Walker's face, the pity, made it all come back, shredding her heart just a little more. She covered her face with her hands when she couldn't stop herself from breaking down again. It wasn't just crying. She was one of those ridiculously noisy, messy criers who snorted and hiccuped. "I'm sorry," she cried out as she felt the sofa cushion dip, his arm slipping around her, and he just let her sob.

Chapter 25

Walker had been freaking out. How could he not, with Kate not picking up her phone? He had learned what that prick Weber and his partner, Medina, had done. Basically, they had taken their very helpful witness and tossed her under the bus as would every other cop out there. Assholes!

He'd tracked her cell phone. Totally illegal, which he knew, but this was Kate, and after learning she no longer worked at the hotel, Walker was thinking some pretty bad thoughts. After tracking her down at home, he'd summoned the super to let him in. The guy had hesitated only a second before Walker showed his badge and advised him that Kate was his girlfriend and most likely in a pretty bad way—a long shot, and he made a mental note to tell Kate she should move as soon as the short balding man shoved his key into the lock and let Walker in anyway.

Now he just rubbed her back, taking in the ice cream in the tub, the mess around her. He didn't have a clue how to start to fix this for her. "I'm sorry. Weber met with your boss, and I'm afraid he let out that you accessed guest information, showed the details you provided. I was worried something had happened, and I called the hotel, and they said you no longer worked there."

Her face was still buried into his chest, and she was now a sobbing mess. "It was horrible," she choked out. "Tony hates me, and I can't believe your cop friends went in and showed him what I provided. You gave them those folios. The whole entire thing was twisted around to make me look like the bad guy, as if I did something wrong. Tony didn't seem to care that Jamie and his wife did what they did. It was more about me giving out the guest information, as if helping the police was a crime. It made no sense..."

She was going on and on, which Kate tended to do when she got worked up. Any other time he would have stopped her, but now he just said, "Shh, it's okay."

"No, it's not okay." She pulled away. Her face was red and blotchy, her eyes swollen, and she was furious. "Why did those detectives talk to Tony? Why did they mention I helped? Why would they do such a thing? I helped them, you. Why did you pass the folios on to those jerks?"

What could he say to get her to understand that those pricks were just doing what any cop would have done, what he would have done if the witness had been someone else? "This is why I didn't want you helping, Kate. This is why I wanted you far away from them and not involved in this at all. The truth, Kate, is that Tony shut them down and refused any more access or help, which makes us suspicious. I'm sorry, but the moment you went in and printed off those documents, I couldn't keep them from Weber and Medina. They were evidence."

Kate had moved back and was sitting up on the sofa, pulling wads of Kleenex from the box, blowing her nose, wiping. "I don't understand. Why isn't he angry about

Jamie and Tess?" She reached forward and smacked his shoulder. "And why did you let your cop friends do that? I walked into it this afternoon. Do you have any idea how horrible it was to be treated so badly? I don't even think Keith expected it," she said, dabbing at her eyes with the Kleenex again.

"They're not my friends, Kate." No, he'd really pushed the night before to keep her out of it, so much so that even his boss had stepped in, as Kate had been so willing to be helpful. He knew she had done it for him.

"Listen, why don't we go out for dinner or..." He stopped when she flashed him a *Hell, no, are you completely insane?* look. She didn't have to say a word for him to know he wasn't talking her into setting one foot out the door.

"I'm not hungry," she said. "I just downed a ridiculous amount of ice cream, and it's not sitting too well."

He glanced at the tub and wondered if all women were the emotional types to drown their sorrows in ice cream. He was about to ask when he took in Kate and the anger flashing his way. Maybe it would be best if he didn't comment on that. "Come on," he said. "I think it will do you good to get out."

She appeared to have no intention of moving, however. In fact, she crossed her arms as he slid his hand over the blanket she had tossed over her legs. "Do I look like I want to go out? No, Walker, you go. I'm staying here. I have no desire to run into anyone, to see anyone. I want to just lie here and lick my wounds and figure out what's next. Oh, God, who's going to hire me now? They'll ask why I left my last job, and I'll have to tell them I was fired. Oh, this is awful." Then she started crying again, and Walker wanted to seriously hurt both Weber and Medina.

Chapter 26

I t was three a.m., and Kate was still awake.

Walker had left about three hours before after insisting on ordering pizza, meat lover's with extra cheese. She'd had two pieces, and he'd even popped down to the corner to grab a six pack of beer. She'd gladly had one, and although she wasn't a beer drinker, she'd found it went nicely with the greasy, heavy pizza, which only added to the burning in her stomach from the ice cream. That was probably why she now felt a hefty twenty pounds heavier. She'd moped about it and hadn't much felt like having sex with Walker, not that he'd pushed. That was something Walker would never do. Really, having sex and sharing any part of herself in an intimate way was just something she couldn't do right now.

Maybe he'd understood, as she'd caught him several times looking across the room at her, watching her as he took another swallow from his beer. The look he had while sitting across from her made her wonder whether he was now figuring out how to cut his losses. Could she blame him?

She'd have to think about that, but then, all she'd been doing was thinking. Walker had said he was staying over and had slid into bed beside her without sex, pulling her against him to lie there, which she had to admit had been somewhat comforting, but then his phone had rung not more than fifteen minutes later. He'd had to go because there had been another crime. She noted that seemed to only happen at night. Walker had dressed and left, and she wondered whether maybe he was relieved, but that thought alone added another slice to the open wound in her heart, so here she was in bed, alone, thinking—and that wasn't a good thing.

It was times like this, when her life had turned to shit, that she should never ever be alone with her thoughts, thoughts that had her reliving every painful, horrible event that had happened and then adding a few extra twists and worries to turn a really bad situation into something resembling hopelessness.

"Stop it," she said with a groan, pressing her hands to her face. She finally sat up and threw back the covers to slip from bed and pull on a T-shirt. She flicked on the bedside light, reached for her heavy terrycloth red housecoat, and pulled it on, then added a pair of wool socks before wandering out into the living room and turning on the lamp on the sofa table. She started cleaning up the leftover pizza box, from which Walker had polished off the last piece. The man could eat, she had to give him that.

She moved the empties to the kitchen counter, her one beer to Walker's two. Then she stood there, exhausted and drained but wired, unable to sleep. Every time she laid her head down, it started thinking, so she did the only thing she could think of: She pulled out her MacBook Pro, fired it up, gave herself a quick talking to, and started updating her resume.

She needed references. Her hands were shaking and her insides jittery from the five cups of coffee she'd downed. She had talked to five different hoteliers since the clock hit eight a.m., and each one had asked for her resume, which she'd immediately sent by email, but she needed references. That was going to be a problem of sorts, one that had made her literally pull out her hair.

Hollis, the head of security, had already replied to her email saying yeah, he'd say a few good things about her. She already knew he liked her, though. Tony…well, she knew he'd make sure she never worked anywhere, so she hadn't bothered reaching out to him. Jeanette, who was the head of food and beverage, would have to pass, she said in her email, only because she wouldn't want to rock the boat with Tony. Then, of course, there were the Prescotts, the owners of the hotel. Kate didn't really know what side of the fence they sat on. If they were on her side, she'd have a job back. If not, it might be best not to rock that boat. Then there was Keith. After what he'd said to her the day before when she left, she sensed maybe an ally, an unusual one—or maybe not. He was an odd unhappy man who thrived on misery.

Maybe because she was so wired and overtired, she didn't think as she dialed the phone. It rang once before it was answered by a young female voice she didn't recognize. She asked for Keith, and the friendly girl transferred him.

"Keith Drummond." He sounded distracted.

"It's Kate. I hope you don't mind me calling?" she said, shutting her eyes and wincing. Keith had been the person at the hotel who'd made her job difficult.

"No, no, you're probably wondering about your last

check." He cleared his throat, and she could hear paper rustling in the background.

"Well, yes, I am, but that isn't why I'm calling. I'm applying for other jobs, and they need references. I just want to ask, because I've always worked hard, done a good job, and I want to see if you'll give me a fair shake with a reference."

What was the worst he could say, *I'm going to say every-thing bad about you so that you never work in this industry ever again?* Then she'd know, and then what? She'd down another pot of coffee and come up with plan D.

There was a sound in the background as if he were tapping a pen or pencil on the desk, and then she heard a door shut. "Listen, Kate, I feel real bad about what happened to you. I never knew Jamie was doing what he was doing, and we've had the Prescotts here today breathing down Tony's neck, demanding answers. I'm kind of lying low, trying to stay out of the line of fire. They're worried about the publicity and news getting out that guests who stayed here were getting robbed by hotel staff even though it was one guy. It's bad. I feel for you, Kate."

She'd never taken a moment to think about it. Jamie had worked under her, as well, and she had never seen it, never suspected. "So you never suspected anything like this was happening? I mean, not one of those guests said a word about being robbed?"

There was more tapping in the background. "I shouldn't be saying this, Kate." Keith had lowered his voice as if making sure no one would hear him. "Those guests who were robbed…I overheard Brian Prescott speaking with Tony, asking whether he was aware of hookers coming into the hotel, asking questions about how staff could get away with this."

"Was he? I mean, did Tony know? I remember that

one incident I told you about, that guest who approached that poor lady in the lobby waiting for her dinner companion. The guy hurried off, but I wondered whether you or Tony spoke with him."

There was silence for a moment.

"Keith? Was there more to it?" she asked.

"No, no, I let Tony know about it. It was for him to handle, and he said to just let it go. I thought nothing of it, considering the man checked out the next day. Hey, listen, Kate. I'm really sorry about what happened. If you have me down for a reference, I won't tell anyone what happened, but I also have a friend down in Sacramento who manages a smaller hotel. I could put a call in to him, see if he's hiring."

Sacramento! She lived here in Portland. Her parents were here, she had grown up here…Walker was here. "Thanks, but I think I'll keep trying here."

"Okay, but if you change your mind, let me know."

After she hung up, she was surprised at Keith's response, at him being so nice. He'd never been the entire time she had worked there. Maybe he really did feel bad about what had happened. Maybe this wasn't as hopeless as she'd thought.

Chapter 27

It had been two days since he'd left Kate's, and he was still wearing the same shirt. He really needed to call her to see how she was. This was the first time he'd been around a woman on the edge, and he hadn't once considered running or finding a way to cut ties and move on. Maybe that was because he couldn't help but blame himself for her problems.

"Wow, you look like crap. Have you been home at all?" Kruso said. She appeared refreshed, dropping her cloth purse on her desk and then opening the bottom drawer to dump it in.

"No. Solved the case, though. Caught a break, a fluke, really. The crazy motherfucker was actually the nephew. What is it with family? I wonder sometimes." He looked over to Kruso, who was sitting, pulling her chair up.

"Then go home, get some rest, shower, change. You talk to Kate?"

He wondered why Kruso kept asking about Kate. He was pretty sure this wasn't something she did with everyone. He shook his head, and then he could hear her tsking under her breath. He shot another glance her way, standing up and stretching. He was stiff and needed a hot shower. "I should call her."

"Yes, you should. I take it she hasn't called you?" Now she was starting to sound like a mother.

"She's a big girl. She knows I'm working."

"You're a little thick sometimes, Walker. You should call her now, check in, especially after what happened, losing her job because of your investigation. Her head is probably not in a good space."

It was a bitter pill to swallow. In the end, Weber and Medina had both said they figured the GM had known about the hookers, and they suspected but couldn't prove that he may have been letting Jamie arrange them for the men, the guests, while looking the other way. But Jamie wasn't talking, and he and his wife had taken a plea because of Tony's lawyer, a good lawyer who was keen to shut this entire investigation down and keep it quiet so the hotel could go on with business as usual.

"Hey, I didn't walk out on her. I stayed with her. Couldn't do much to cheer her up, though. Geez, do all women drown their sorrows in ice cream?" He glanced over to Kruso, whose expression changed. She looked up and gestured with her chin.

"Kate's here," she said.

He turned to see her standing at the edge of the squad room in her black and white coat and blue jeans, looking around. "Kate, what are you doing here?" He was walking toward her as she stepped around some cops, heading his way. Her expression was off. He wasn't sure what to make of it.

"Hey, I hope I'm not bothering you," she said. She seemed so tense, holding back a piece of herself like she hadn't before. This wasn't his hot, sexy, responsive Kate.

"No, of course not. Was just about to call you. I'm sorry, I got wrapped up in this case."

Her hand went to his shirt before she squeezed her fist and shoving it in her pocket. "You've been here the entire time? You look tired."

"I am, and yes, sorry, it was just one of those cases. A lead came, and we got the guy. It's done. How are you doing?" He reached up to her shoulder and touched her, taking in the other cops watching them. "Come on, let's go into the break room for a little privacy."

He reached for her hand. There was hesitation, which made him take another look at her. It was then that he saw her force a smile, and he let her go. She was stiff and hadn't slipped her hand into his as he'd expected.

She followed him into the break room, which was empty, thankfully. He gestured to a chair and wondered why he was being so polite. She shook her head again, so tight, on edge. Then she folded her hands together in front of her as if she needed that distraction, standing so straight.

"What's going on? You seem upset, off, distracted. Which is it?"

"All of the above. I don't know how to say this." Her big bold eyes were filled with such sadness that he knew he wasn't going to like what she said.

"Just say it. Don't beat around the bush. What's going on?"

"I'm leaving. I can't stay in Portland. I have a job offer —or rather Keith made a call and got me a job down in Sacramento. A friend of his runs a boutique hotel and has an opening for an assistant. It's the kind of job I've always wanted. Because it's a smaller hotel, I won't be the assistant of just one department. I'll be overseeing the place and doing what I'm good at."

He didn't know what to say. Sacramento, another city. That would take Kate away from here, away from him. "Look, Kate, it's been just a few days. I'm sure there's something here. I'll help you find something."

She was shaking her head as if her mind was made up, and she reached out to touch his arm before stepping forward and up on her toes, kissing his cheek. It was a typical move, not too intimate, but it told him *So long, it's over* without her having to say the words. Then she stepped back, her hands jammed in her pockets again. She looked away as if she needed space and distance. "No, I've had time to think, and I think this would be for the best. Give me a fresh start, a new place."

He shrugged. "And us, Kate? What about you and me?"

Then she smiled, but it was a sad smile, and her eyes seemed to be a little shiny. Maybe it was the light, but he thought she was trying not to cry. "Oh, Walker, you really believe there's a you and me and it's not just about the sex?" She was shaking her head again. "Just think of it as me saving you from eventually looking for a way to get out, to break away from me. I mean, two days you were here without a word to me, and I got a pretty good idea after no calls, not hearing from you, that you need this more than me. It's okay, I'm not mad, but I need more, so I'm taking the job in Sacramento." She nodded and went to turn away.

He didn't know what to say to her. It made him furious to have her toss him to the curb this way, to have her think he thought so little of her. "Kate, I had a case! I can't call when I get wrapped up in solving it. I'm sorry. Why don't you understand it had nothing to do with me trying to get rid of you? You really think so little of me?"

She was shaking her head, her brow furrowed. "No, it's

the opposite, really. I fear my feelings for you are so much that you'll end up destroying me. Maybe I'm the one who's not strong enough here. Maybe it's me. I understand how you give everything you have of yourself to do your job. It's one of the things I love about you, your dedication, but I also know I'll be second—and I can't be second, Walker." She held up her hand as she stepped back again. "I'm sorry, Walker. I really am."

She left before he could say anything else. He could have gone after her. He could have talked her out of it, changed her mind. He knew he was strong willed enough that he could make her see things his way, but Walker Pruett never chased after any woman, and as he stood alone in the coffee room, he reminded himself that he wasn't about to start now.

Chapter 28

She was packed. She'd had a goodbye dinner the night before with her parents even though Sacramento wasn't that far and she'd probably end up seeing them more than she did living in the same city. She was excited about the move after renting a cute little apartment a few blocks from work and talking with Ted Mueller, the current GM, who seemed nice, pleasant. How could he be friends with Keith? An anomaly, maybe.

Since she was in a lease, she had decided to sublet a furnished apartment. It had been easier than she'd thought, and what she wouldn't take with her she would store in her parents' garage. She'd also purchased a small compact, which was loaded up with everything and was parked downstairs, waiting for her. She took one last look around, locked up her apartment, and dropped off her keys with the super downstairs, who would give them to the young couple moving in later that afternoon. Even though she was sad about leaving so many things, she realized she was making a new start, and she needed to be excited about it.

She didn't see him right away.

He was leaning against her car, wearing dark shades, dress pants, and a white shirt. His tie was loosened, and he hadn't shaved, from the looks of it, for days. It was such a messy look that made him damn attractive.

"Walker, I—uh…" She didn't know what the hell to say. This was awkward. She'd said goodbye to him at the station. Why was he prolonging this?

"What you said at the station to me was absolute bullshit, Kate," Walker said. He wasn't one to sugarcoat anything, always right to the point, shocking her from the moment she'd met him. His arms were crossed.

She didn't know how to respond. She started, but nothing came out.

"Don't deny it. You know shit about how I feel, and you must think pretty badly of me to think or assume that I would be relieved in some way about you leaving. Running, really? I think it's you who's scared. I told you I was in, I want you, but when something bad happened, instead of staying and working through it, you up and ran."

Wait, he had it all wrong. "That's not true, Walker. Sooner or later you would have found a way to walk away. I got fired, and you were gone for—"

"I had a case. I'm sorry, but that doesn't mean you're second. I'm a cop. That's who I am, and I'm damn good at what I do, but in no way does me working a job mean I don't care or that you're an afterthought. You're the one who's scared," he said again, and this time he slipped off his glasses and stepped away from the car until he was looking right down at her with those amazing eyes. He wasn't pulling away, turning away, or running away.

"Walker, I have a job in Sacramento now. I have to work. I sublet an apartment. Maybe you're right, maybe it's me, but it's not because I don't want you. I'm scared because I want you so bad and I fell for you so hard. It terrifies me that I'll let slip how much you got in here, that I have feelings for you. I'm falling in love with you, and me telling you may just be the cue for you to panic and walk away."

He was shaking his head, his face lower. "Did you ever stop to think, Kate, that maybe, just maybe, I have those feelings for you, too?"

He couldn't. It couldn't be possible. Then his hand was on her arm, her shoulder, and maybe she shivered, unable to resist his touch. He had to know.

"Don't go, Kate," he said.

"What about my job?" she replied, sliding her hand over his chest, splaying her fingers out until she could feel his heart beating.

"There're other jobs, Kate. Take your time here. I'll help," he said, his hand still holding her, his other sliding over her hip, over the back pocket of her jeans.

"I don't have a place to live now. I rented a place in Sacramento."

He was smiling now in that cocky way of his. "Yeah, but I have a place, a house, and you may as well just move in with me," he said, and she wanted to roll her eyes. When he looked down at her, his expression this time turned serious. "I mean it, Kate, you and me. Come on, let's go home and figure this thing out together."

It was a moment, a choice to go or stay, to dig deep and decide what it was she really wanted.

"What's it going to be, Kate?" he asked.

When she looked up to him and really saw him, the real Walker, who was, in this moment, opening this door and letting her in, she knew she wanted this. She needed to be strong enough to grab it and hold on to it with both hands, so she held up the keys to the compact and set them in Walker's palm.

"So are you driving?" she said.

He took her keys and her hand as he reached down and opened the passenger door. "Just so you know, the pool table in the dining room stays," he said as she slid into the car. He shut the door and walked around to the driver's side, and Kate wondered about the fun, about how long it would take her to wear him down until she could start adding touches to his man cave. If it was up to her, it would soon begin to resemble a home a normal couple would have.

Turn the page for a sneak peek of
LAST NIGHT the next book in the *KATE & WALKER* series.
Available in print, audio & eBook

—"Romantic suspense at its best...This book was a quick read but was not short on the emotional suspense and family drama for which Eckhart is known. Her characters are always so real and raw. The plot is interesting and keeps the pages turning. The alpha hero keeps the pages steaming."

AHERMAN

"Two weeks of craziness."

SUSAN

— "Just when you think they will have their HEA, a scheming, conniving woman throws a huge monkey wrench into their plans."

VEGGIEGIRL55

The adventure continues for Kate & Walker in LAST NIGHT as Walker proposes marriage to Kate realizing he can't live without her. Only an intruder from Walker's past puts both Kate's life and his relationship with her, in jeopardy.

Last Night

CHAPTER 1

The glitter staring back at Kate from the velvet green box had her bringing her hand to her chest, doing her very best to breathe and make sense of what she was looking at.

"Aren't you going to answer me?" Walker asked. He was now seated across from her at a small window table for two at a local Italian restaurant in a part of town where she'd never been. The tablecloth was white, the dinnerware was silver, and the atmosphere was cozy. Then there was Walker, who was such a contrast to this place. As Kate took in the men seated by the door, though—their dark hair and olive skin, their suits, their concrete expressions— she realized maybe Walker did fit in, after all.

Her other hand was in her lap, pressed against her blue jeans, and she was feeling warm in her black turtleneck. Walker had just finished at the precinct and was dressed in dark dress pants and a suit jacket, the two top buttons of his white dress shirt undone. He looked dashing tonight, sexy as hell. She loved watching him. As her gaze flicked up to his deep green eyes, something in his expression had her throat closing up again. Her hand was shaking as she touched her chest once more and tucked her shoulder-length hair behind her ears. She'd recently had foils done to bring out a lighter shade, a hint of auburn.

"Kate, you're making me kind of nervous, here. I just asked you to marry me, and with you not answering, I'm starting to wonder if maybe I already have my answer." He was starting to sound defensive—no, mad, and she was still trying to figure out what the hell was going on.

She shut her eyes for a second to give herself a mental shake. "Stop," she said, holding up her hand. "I just need a second, Walker. You walk in here after telling me to meet you for dinner at this address and leaving me waiting for twenty minutes, and then you just dump this box in front of me. And, just for the record, you didn't ask me to marry you. I opened the box, and I suppose—"

He rolled his eyes as if she was creating a problem where one didn't exist. "What did you think I was giving you? It's an engagement ring, Kate. What did you think it meant?" He gestured to it as if he was the sane one and she was supposed to just read his mind.

What was he thinking? Was he serious? She actually had to place her hands on the tabletop, as she wanted to reach across and smack him. Walker was anything but easy, and at times like this he had her wanting to pull her hair out. "You need to use your words, Walker," she said as she somehow found the nerve to close the ring box and move it across the table in front of him. She set it down with a hard smack. "Ask me nicely, because I want to hear you grovel and treat me the way a woman should be treated. Ask me the way a man should when he wants to marry a woman, not just by showing up late and tossing me a ring as if this is just another task you're glad to be done with. That…" She pointed to him and the ring, which was now hidden from view. From her first glance, it had been a stunning ring.

"You want me down on my knees," he said, though he didn't appear any closer to doing just that. In fact, he was leaning back in his chair, giving her the impression that she was being ridiculous.

When the waiter appeared beside her, she smiled brightly at him, lifting her menu, which she'd studied from front to back four times, given how long she'd waited for Walker since ordering a glass of chianti to start.

"Are you ready to order?" the young Italian man asked.

"No," Walker said at the same time Kate said, "Yes."

She glanced up to the waiter, who seemed to hesitate as he slowly looked up from his notepad over to her and then Walker, maybe realizing he had walked in on something he should have backed away from.

"Why don't I give you a few more minutes?" he said, and before Kate could contradict Walker again, the waiter hurried away.

"Walker, seriously, let's order dinner. I'm starving, and I've been waiting here for you, which seems to be the story of my life." She'd lost count of the number of dinners she'd eaten alone because something had come up and Walker hadn't made it home. After the first dozen times, she'd started texting him whenever she decided to cook up something nice, which was several times a week now, since she still didn't have a job and had all this free time. She'd found that in order to save her sanity, she needed to text him a reminder that (A) dinner was ready and (B) she'd been cooking for hours for him. That seemed to be what he needed to at least come home and eat, knowing she was going to some trouble for him.

Walker crossed his arms, narrowing his gaze as if determined to wait her out. "No, I want an answer," he said. "Do you have any idea what I've put out there?" He lifted the ring box. "This rock I bought for you, Kate, my ring that I want on your finger…this is a huge step."

"And maybe one you're not ready for," she couldn't help adding, because he didn't seem to be any closer to getting on his knees and saying the words she wanted—no, needed to hear.

He seemed to be thinking, considering, maybe, as he stared at her in that dark way of his that let her know she was pushing him further than was wise. Walker was a man with many complex sides, far from easy, far from predictable—especially when he was screwing her brains out, riding her hard and fast. That was when she saw his dominant side, not that Walker wasn't a very masculine male. He was, being a cop who saw the dark side of everything. Bossiness was just another side of him, and getting Walker to see her way was akin to moving mountains, at times. So it really was no wonder that she had to fight the urge to rap her head against the table as she stared back at him this time, not willing to give an inch. As she lifted her hand to get the waiter's attention, she heard the scrape of a chair.

Walker was standing, pulling on his jacket as he walked around to her.

"What are you doing?" She was nervous now. Walker had just thrown her for a loop. She didn't know what he was doing, and that was freaking her out. She looked around to see interest from the waiter and the few tables of men turned their way.

He didn't say a word as he stood in front of her, set the ring box back on the table, and went down on one knee.

"Walker, it's okay. Get up," she said. The other men were smiling at the scene Walker was making.

"No. You want the whole shebang, and that's what

you're getting. Kate, my darling, my sweetheart, I would like very much to marry you, to make you my wife, who'll torment me and test my patience…"

There were a few laughs from the other table, and she couldn't help shooting a glare their way as she lifted her chin. When she glanced over to Walker, he wasn't smiling but watching her, waiting.

"That was about the worst proposal I've ever heard," she said.

He stood up, opened the ring box again, pulled the ring out, and reached for her hand. She allowed him to slip it on her finger as she took in the six diamonds, not large and gauche but square, simple. It looked fantastic on her finger.

"Just say yes. Come on, Kate. You know you want to."

She tried to look mad. She wanted him to finish, to add in some terms of endearment, to say how much he couldn't live without her, that he'd love her forever—but as soon as the thought crossed her mind, she had to toss it away. Walker was not a man for sentiments or flowery words, and as she stared at the ring on her finger and back to the man who'd turned her life and emotions and world upside down, she knew she'd never want him to be.

So she took a deep breath and made him wait a little longer than she needed to just because she enjoyed driving him to the edge, making him a little crazy for her. When she heard him swear under his breath, she smiled and said, "I'll think about it."

About the Author

"Lorhainne Eckhart is one of my go to authors when I want a guaranteed good book. So many twists and turns, but also so much love and such a strong sense of family."

(LORA W., REVIEWER)

New York Times & USA Today bestseller Lorhainne Eckhart is best known for writing Raw Relatable Real Romance where "Morals and family are running themes." As one fan calls her, she is the "Queen of the family saga." (aherman) writing "the ups and downs of what goes on within a family but also with some suspense, angst and of course a bit of romance thrown in for good measure."

Follow Lorhainne on Bookbub to receive alerts on New Releases and Sales and join her mailing list at Lorhainne-Eckhart.com for her Monday Blog, all book news, give-aways and FREE reads. With over 120 books, audiobooks, and multiple series published and available at all, retailers now translated into six languages. She is a multiple recipient of the Readers' Favorite Award for Suspense and Romance, and lives in the Pacific Northwest on an island, is the mother of three, her oldest has autism and she is an advocate for never giving up on your dreams.

"Lorhainne Eckhart has this uncanny way of just hitting the spot every time with her books."

(CAROLINE L., REVIEWER)

The O'Connells: *The O'Connells of Livingston, Montana are not your typical family. A riveting collection of stories surrounding the ups and downs of what goes on within a family but also with some suspense, angst and of course a bit of romance thrown in for good measure. "I thought I loved the Friessens, but I absolutely adore the O'Connell's. Each and every book has different genres of stories, but the one thing in common is how she is able to wrap it around the family, which is the heart of each story." (C. Logue)*

The Friessens: *An emotional big family romance series, the Friessen family siblings find their relationships tested, lay their hearts on the line, and discover lasting love! "Lorhainne Eckhart is one of my go to authors when I want* *a guaranteed good book. So many twists and turns, but also so much love and such a strong sense of family." (Lora W., Reviewer)*

The Parker Sisters: *The Parker Sisters are a close-knit family, and like any other family they have their ups and downs. Eckhart has crafted another intense family drama… "The character development is outstanding, and the emotional investment is high…" (Aherman, Reviewer)*

The McCabe Brothers: *Join the five McCabe siblings on their journeys to the dark and dangerous side of love! An intense, exhilarating collection of romantic thrillers you won't want to miss. — "Eckhart has a new series that is definitely worth the read. The queen of the family saga started this series with a spin-off of her wildly successful Friessen series." From a Readers' Favorite award—winning author and "queen of the family saga" (Aherman)*

Billy Jo McCabe Mystery: *The social worker and the cop, an unlikely couple drawn together on a small, secluded Pacific Northwest island where nothing is as it seems. Protecting the innocent comes at a cost, and what seems to be a sleepy, quiet town is anything but.*

Lorhainne loves to hear from her readers! You can connect with me at:
www.LorhainneEckhart.com
lorhainneeckhart.le@gmail.com

 facebook.com/AuthorLorhainneEckhart

twitter.com/LEckhart

instagram.com/lorhainneeckhart

bookbub.com/profile/lorhainne-eckhart

pinterest.com/lorhainneeckhart

Also by Lorhainne Eckhart

The Outsider Series
The Forgotten Child (Brad and Emily)
A Baby and a Wedding *(An Outsider Series Short)*
Fallen Hero (Andy, Jed, and Diana)
The Awakening (Andy and Laura)
Secrets (Jed and Diana)
Runaway (Andy and Laura)
Overdue *(An Outsider Series Short)*
The Unexpected Storm (Neil and Candy)
The Wedding (Neil and Candy)

The Friessens: A New Beginning
The Deadline (Andy and Laura)
The Price to Love (Neil and Candy)
A Different Kind of Love (Brad and Emily)
A Vow of Love, A Friessen Family Christmas

The Friessens
The Reunion
The Bloodline (Andy & Laura)
The Promise (Diana & Jed)
The Business Plan (Neil & Candy)
The Decision (Brad & Emily)
First Love (Katy)
Family First
Leave the Light On
In the Moment
In the Family
In the Silence

In the Charm
Unexpected Consequences
It Was Always You
The First Time I Saw You
Welcome to My Arms
Welcome to Boston
I'll Always Love You
Ground Rules
A Reason to Breathe
You Are My Everything
Anything For You
The Homecoming
Stay Away From My Daughter
The Bad Boy
A Place of Our Own
The Visitor
All About Devon
Long Past Dawn
How to Heal a Heart
Keep Me In Your Heart

The O'Connells
The Neighbor
The Third Call
The Secret Husband
The Quiet Day
The Commitment
The Missing Father
The Hometown Hero
Justice
The Family Secret
The Fallen O'Connell
The Return of the O'Connells
And The She Was Gone

The Stalker
The O'Connell Family Christmas
The Girl Next Door
Broken Promises
The Gatekeeper
The Hunted

The McCabe Brothers

Don't Stop Me (Vic)
Don't Catch Me (Chase)
Don't Run From Me (Aaron)
Don't Hide From Me (Luc)
Don't Leave Me (Claudia)
Out of Time

A Billy Jo McCabe Mystery

Nothing As it Seems
Hiding in Plain Sight
The Cold Case
The Trap
Above the Law
The Stranger at the Door
The Children
The Last Stand
The Charity
The Sacrifice

The Street Fighter

Finding Home

The Wilde Brothers

The One (Joe and Margaret)
The Honeymoon, A Wilde Brothers Short
Friendly Fire (Logan and Julia)

Not Quite Married, A Wilde Brothers Short
A Matter of Trust (Ben and Carrie)
The Reckoning, A Wilde Brothers Christmas
Traded (Jake)
Unforgiven (Samuel)
The Holiday Bride

Married in Montana
His Promise
Love's Promise
A Promise of Forever

The Parker Sisters
Thrill of the Chase
The Dating Game
Play Hard to Get
What We Can't Have
Go Your Own Way
A June Wedding

Kate & Walker
One Night
Edge of Night
Last Night

Walk the Right Road Series
The Choice
Lost and Found
Merkaba
Bounty
Blown Away: The Final Chapter
He Came Back

The Saved Series

Saved
Vanished
Captured

Single Titles
Loving Christine